Copyright © 2017 Chrissy O

All rights reserved

The characters and events portrayed in this book are fictitious. Any similarity to real persons, living or dead, is coincidental and not intended by the author.

No part of this book may be reproduced, or stored in a retrieval system, or transmitted in any form or by any means, electronic, mechanical, photocopying, recording, or otherwise, without express written permission of the publisher.

CONTENTS

Copyright	1
Chapter 1: Questions	5
Chapter 2: Killing Season	11
Chapter 3: I'm Home	15
Chapter 4: I See Dead People	21
Chapter 5: I want out	28
Chapter 6: You're Never Alone	35
Chapter 7: A Dream Come True	44
Chapter 8: There's A Snake In The Grass	54
Chapter 9: I'm Not To Be Played With	67
Chapter 10: Family Problems	86
Chapter 11: Death Is Never The Answer	97
Chapter 12: The Day The Earth Stood Still	105
Chapter 13: Dreams Do Come True	116
Chapter 14: A True Diva	124
Chapter 15: This Is It	135
Epilogue	141

I Fell In Love With The Plug 3
The End Of The Lies

By: Chrissy O.

CHAPTER 1: QUESTIONS
Zack

POP!!! POP!!! Was all that could be heard throughout the warehouse. I put a bullet into Javier left and right knee. The fact that he still wasn't talking was making everyone mad. I put on a pair of brass knuckles and delivered deadly blows onto his face until his left eye was swollen shut. I knocked out 5 of his teeth and dislocated his jaw in the process. "You have the wrong on. I'm just following order," he whispered. I noticed no one heard him so I waited until everyone left to finish him up.

As I stood over Javier the comment he made had me second guessing on killing him right now. He said he wasn't the one out to get Brooke he was just following orders. He said it so low I almost missed it until I asked him what the fuck did he just say. I wanted to make his death slow and painful but now I couldn't. When he asked me to help him I knew I had no choice because this shit wouldn't end until we found out who was the cause of all of this.

I knew the second I agreed to do this shit with Javier it would come back and bite me in my ass but I wasn't going to let him take Lucas down. The plan was to figure out who the inside person was and to dead them before they could get to Brooklyn. I knew she lived a crazy life coming up but for some reason someone wanted her dead and I needed to know why. I mean why target a kid who probably knows nothing of her father's stash. I mean I could be wrong but until Javier gives me the answers that I want can't kill him yet.

When Lucas left the warehouse I helped clean Javier up and took him back to my house to see what all information he would give me. He didn't give me much at first because he was in a lot of pain. I had to call Dr. Ali so they he could fix him up before he ended up dead and then I would never found out who's behind these hits on Brooklyn. A couple of days went by before Javier finally woke up and when he did I got straight down to business. He wouldn't give me much detail but the little information he did give me I took it and ran with it.

I felt like the dirtiest friend on Earth right now. I wanted to warn Lucas so bad but the fact that he said he would find out if I did made me really wonder who the inside person was tipping him off and giving him information. The team we ran with was small but they had a lot of works under them so it could be anyone yapping off at the mouth. I needed answers and I needed them now. "Why are you so eager to kill Brooke? She ain't do shit to you so why won't you leave her alone?" I asked him as I passed him a cup of cold water.

"See that's where you're wrong my friend. Did you forget who her father was? That girl has more blood on her hands then any of you even know. He father trained her to be the best, but she acts as if she doesn't know shit," Javier told me while sipping from his cup.

At that point I wondered who else had she killed and what had she killed them for. "Well here's my burner phone if you decide to tell me anything else," I told him as I tossed the phone into his lap.

"I will tell you everything only if you agree to help me take back my throne," he said. I turned to look at him as if he was speaking a foreign language.

I rubbed the side of my face, took a long breath, and said, "What do I have to do?" I feel like I just sold my soul to the devil because I just knew how my life was going to end.

"I will be in touch," he said as he waived the burner phone at me. I took that as my cue to get up and leave. I hoped this shit went the way I wanted it to but I knew it wasn't. I had him tucked away in my condo that nobody knew about. I was suppose to had given it to Sade once she graduated from school but our relationship was so rocky lately I was just going to wait. When I got to my car I pulled out a fat blunt and smoked my stress and worries away.

A part of me wanted to be man enough to tell Lucas what I was up too but a part of me said to stay low key and not let him know just in case Javier was playing me. I picked up my phone and quickly called Sade because I needed to relieve this stress before I had more blood then I needed on my hands right now. "So you think you're just going to call me when you went missing on me all night Zackery," Sade yelled into the phone the second she picked it up.

"Look bitch don't start I had fucking work to do. Where the fuck you at?" I asked while headed to her house.

"At home in the bed where I always am when I'm not with you or the girls," she stated which I knew was true. I hung the phone up because I was not about to argue with her.

When I pulled up to her house she was standing in the window with no clothes on which lets me know that her mother wasn't home. I used my key to let myself in and went straight to her room. Within seconds she had my shaft down her throat sucking the kids right out of me.

"SHHHHHHHIT!!!!!! I said while I started to fuck her face. I loved Sade because she was a freak and did whatever I wanted. I had been smashing her since I meet her and sometimes I felt like she would be my downfall because the pussy was that good.

"Let me taste that," I told her while licking my lips and putting her down on the bed.

"Go right ahead daddy," she said while spreading eagle and played with herself that only made me even more horny. I gripped her thighs and pulled her towards my face and went to town. The only thing that could be heard in the room was my lips smacking up against her pretty pussy lips and the moans that escaped her mouth.

With the two fingers I inserted inside of her had her running away from the head. "Bring that ass back here," I demanded her while I buried my mouth deeper in her pussy. The strokes my tongue delivered to her kitty had her trembling. I came up for air and tossed her over onto her knees. I sucked on her kitty from behind and came instantly.

"That's my girl I told her as I licked her clean then entered her from behind.

Her ass clapping against my thighs could be heard down the

street because I was determined to leave her sleeping the next few days.

"Yes baby right there," she told me as I speed up and drilled into her even harder. She had the perfect arch going on and I went even deeper inside of her.

"Who own the pussy," I asked while grabbing a hand full of hair and pulling it back.

"You own it, it's yours," she cried. I pulled out of her and released my kids onto her back. After we cleaned up we feel into a deep sleep. I really had come over to tell her what was going on but that would just have to wait until the morning.

The next morning I tried to sneak out before Sade woke up but she beat me up this time. I tried to hurry up and go out the back but she was standing in the kitchen with my phone in her hand. "You care to explain why the doctor is sending you updates on a person you were ordered to kill," she demanded. I snatched my phone of her hand and mugged her.

"Stay the fuck out of my phone. It's some funny shit going on right now!"

"Yea, like this disloyalty you're doing behind Lucas back," she said which only pissed me off.

"Bitch look here, that nigga said he ain't the only one out to get Brooke, so I have to see who else is after her and I can't do it with him dead," I barked at her.

The looked on my face let her know I was serious and she tried to calm me down but it was too late. "You know I'm far from a liar don't call my phone at all today and until you learn who the fuck you questioning cause it aint me. Does Brooklyn know you fucked Lucas since you want to talk about disloyalty you stupid bitch," I said then smacked her.

When she started crying I left the house. For her to question my motives she had yet to tell me she was fucking Lucas. I caught them in the act when Brooklyn went missing but I never said anything to Lucas about it because I knew Sade was a hoe and would do anything to get a nut.

My only reason for not going off on him was because he really didn't even know. She drugged him and fucked him. I had to take her to get an abortion because Lucas would've killed her and my dumb ass actually loved this hoe. I should have offed her when she drugged Lucas but she was going to come in handy when I needed to drug whoever else was after Brooklyn.

CHAPTER 2: KILLING SEASON

Brooklyn

The entire time at Lucas birthday dinner I felt like something was not right. The tension in the air was so thick I didn't know if it was me or if something was really wrong. Luc was due to get his biggest shipment of the summer tonight so I figured that's probably what it was so I shook the feeling off and continued to eat. He dropped me and the girls off at the house and went to the warehouse.

Nessa, Sade, and I went into the movie room to watch TV until the boys got back. We ended up watching Drag Me To Hell and of course Sade crybaby as was begging us to watch something else. She didn't really like scary movies and we thought it was the funniest shit ever to watch it anyway just to watch her cry. We were about 20 minutes into the movie before Sade ended up going to sleep.

When I looked over at Nessa she had dozed off to sleep too. I swear I kept hearing footsteps upstairs but I figured I was hearing shit and went right back to the movie. I looked at the time and noticed it couldn't be the boys because they weren't do back to the house for another 45 minutes to an hour. When I heard it again I quickly woke up Nessa and Sade because something was clearly going on.

"Bitch why you wake us up?" Sade asked while rubbing her eyes.

"Y'all don't scream but I think someone is in the house," I whispered to them. That got their full attention because they hopped up quick.

"What do we do?" Nessa asked clearly spooked.

"We need to try and make it to the panic room. It's only two doors down, but I had an escape tunnel put in when we first moved here so come on," I told them as we walked to the back of the movie room. I hit a button on the remote and the wall slide up. When we heard someone trying to open the movie room door I pushed them into the wall and went in right behind them and just as it closed I saw feet coming through the door.

I called Lucas phone back to back but he wasn't answering. I hated to call him when he was working and I usually never did so I prayed and hoped he answered his phone. I led them through the tunnels as we reached the panic room. I saw a Mexican man standing right by the door so I knew once I pushed this button I had to quickly close the door or it would be lights out for us. What a lot of people didn't know was that my dad secretly trained me to be an assassin so I knew at this moment shit was going to change and I just hoped I didn't scare Sade or Nessa. I tried Lucas one more time and when he answered I yelled HELLLLLLLP!!!!! Into the phone before I ended the line.

When I looked over at Sade she was ready to cry. "Ok look I will have to run to the door to shut it so as soon as I push this button push it back and don't push it again until the door is locked. Even if I close it and I am not in the room still don't open it. I will come back in a few and I will be ok I promise," I told them as I pulled my hair up into a bun.

"Just wait until the guys get here," Nessa begged but I wasn't trying to hear it. I looked behind her and grabbed the knife I had hidden in the wall. I looked at my girls and told them it was now or never. I pressed the button and slowly made my way out being real quiet not to tip the man off.

Once I was finally out in the open he still didn't notice me so I took that as my cue to attack him. I grabbed him by his neck and stabbed him repeatedly into his neck and watch him take his last breath. "I'm going to close this door don't open it until you see me on the screen with the guys," I told them as I shut the door. I heard them scream no and I knew that everyone in the house heard them too. I snatched the guns off the lifeless body in front of me and went into the closet to see how many would come into the room.

I had home field advantage because I knew my home like the back of my hand. I went into the circuit box in the closet and cut the power to the entire house. I put on my gun holster and put as many guns as I could on me and made sure they were all loaded and off safety. For some reason cutting people gave me a feeling that Lucas couldn't give me. I grabbed the first knife I used when I caught my first body then made my way into the hall.

As I walked into the hall I could hear the men speaking in a language that I couldn't understand. I slipped into Egypt's room and I ended up knocking over a chair. I ran into the closet and left the door cracked to see who would come in. I screwed the silencer on just as my first victim walked into the room.

SPAT!! SPAT!! That was the sound of my gun as the two bullets hit the man right in the heart. I ran behind the door just as the guys body hit the ground.

Once I realized no one heard him fall I made my way out the room down the hall where I heard gunshots coming from. I looked over the rail and saw Lucas on the ground bleeding out and I lost it at the point. I let my guns ring until I heard a familiar voice.

"Baby girl stop shooting," I heard someone that sounded like my father say.

The tears started to fall as I yelled out, "My father is dead," I dropped three more bodies before my father came into view. Someone let Sade and Nessa out the panic room," was the last thing I said before I fainted.

CHAPTER 3: I'M HOME

Hector

My baby girl bodied three of my best henchmen and that shit had me mad. They knew not to harm her, but when they told her they were there with me she thought it was a lie so she killed them. It wasn't until I finally made myself known, she knew they were telling the truth then she passed out. I knew this was going to happen and this was what I feared. When I found the panic room I let Sade and Nessa out and it's crazy how they still look the same. "Are my eyes playing tricks on me?" Sade said.

She looked at Nessa then back at me and asked, "Are you real?" I couldn't do anything but laugh as I disappeared into the closet. When I found the circuit box I restored the power and came back out the closet to where the girls were.

"Yes I am real now come on Brooklyn passed out and I don't know where anything is at in this house," I told them as we made our way back to the front of the house.

When we made our way back up front I found Brooklyn on the couch laid out being checked on by Dr. Tiffany Nicole Washington. She has been working for me for years and anywhere I go she goes with me. She is also my soon to be wife. "She will be fine, she should come through in about an hour or so" my lovely lady said as I turned to face the girls.

"I will explain everything to you all once she wakes up ok," I told them as they both nodded their head yes.

"Is the baby ok?" I heard Sade ask her.

"What baby?" I turned to ask her.

"She's pregnant," Sade told me as I turned to look at Brooklyn.

My baby was having a baby and I couldn't be more excited. What's even crazier is that she's pregnant and this isn't the life I wanted her to live but I knew I had no other choice with the enemies I had lurking in my backyard at the time. See I had been training her as a kid on how to defend herself and I am so glad it paid off. Most men in my profession wouldn't want their daughters doing what mine done but I needed to make sure that she could defend herself whenever I was not around. That was the main reason why me and her mother had broken up years ago and plus she was also sleeping with my cousin and had 3 kids by his no good ass. The sad part is no one knew we were cousins. I always thought Egypt was mines because she looked so much like Brooke but I never got her tested to find out.

When I walked into a spare room I checked on Lucas and he was doing fine. He was hit in the chest, leg, and arm. When he fell he hit his head on the edge of the steps which caused him to blackout. "How long will he be out for?" I asked my baby.

"Not for long he's in pain but I have medicine for that. I got all the bullets out and stopped the bleeding so it's best we watch him until he wakes up," she told me.

"Alright let me call the cleanup crew I'll be right back," I told her as I went into the living room where my daughter was.

When I called Wanda she thought someone was playing jokes on her until she showed up and saw that it was really me. Once the house was back to normal I set the alarm system and went into the kitchen. I was getting hungry so I had to eat before Brooklyn wakes up and asks me 30 million questions. This really was not how I wanted to come back into her life but from the looks of it I had no choice.

See, about 5 years ago this business was passed down to Lucas from his father when he was gunned down. I knew Lucas needed more training but he seemed to be doing fine before I left. His downfall seemed to be Brooklyn and she wasn't going to like what I was about to do not one bit. Every man has a soft spot and well with his being my daughter I knew I had to train him more before he ends up getting them both killed. Brooke can hold her own weight, it was mainly him who couldn't seem to focus around her. I saw a lot of potential in him but I just needed to bring it out of him.

"Hector I'm going to beat your ass if you don't start explaining shit right fucking now," Brooklyn yelled. I knew her smart mouth would never leave but I see she forgot who the fuck she's talking to. As I made my way back to the living room I grabbed Tiffany so that she could check on her.

"Brooklyn Taylor Johnson don't make me knock your ass into next week. I know I have been gone for a while but I will explain everything. Also, I'm not sure who the fuck you think you're talking but your ass ain't too old to be beat," I threatened her while Tiffany checked on her.

"Sorry daddy," she said in her sweet angelic tone. "I thought you were dead. What happened to you?" she asked me while I took a seat next to her on the couch.

"I will explain it to you later. In the meantime go check on Lucas," I told her.

I looked over at Tiffany who was looking at me as if she saw a ghost.

"Baby what's wrong?" She was looking from me to Brooke then I ended up putting 2 and 2 together.

"Brooke come back her for a minute!" I called out to her.

"Yes daddy!" she yelled coming from out of the kitchen.

"I would like for you to meet someone." When Brooke

screwed her face up I knew this was about to funny.

"I would like for you to meet someone. Brooke this is my fiancé Tiffany. Tiffany this is my daughter Brooklyn but Brooke for short." I couldn't do anything but laugh because one thing Brooke didn't do was share me.

"It's nice to finally get to meet you Brooke," Tiffany said while extending her hand but Brooke wasn't having it. I gave her a quick evil glare and she got with the program quick.

"It's nice to meet you too Ms. Tiffany," she finally said but hugged her instead.

I will admit I spoiled her and she did no wrong in my eyes but now I have to put a stop to it. Yea she might be 18 but I will still snatch her ass right on up. I had a lot of catching up to do with Brooke and I just pray her mother hasn't been putting her through hell. "Brooke how's your mom?" I finally asked her.

"I don't know and to be honest Hector I don't give a shit!" she said. That alone let me know that she had been through some shit. I cursed myself for not keeping a closer eye on her.

"Call me Hector one more time and you won't be able to talk for a week!" Just that quick she sent my blood pressure through the roof.

I loved my daughter but her mouth could not be what it was suppose to be at times. I had to stop myself from smacking her just that quick. "Go check on Lucas," I told her just to get her out of the room. The moment she left I called the one person I had watching over her. My oldest son Hector Jr. had stopped answering my calls months ago which made me come back to town sooner than expected.

Upon my return I learned that Brooklyn was pregnant and Hector Jr. quickly went to the back of my mind. Her health was more important than anything else to me. I figured my son probably didn't want to be found so I left it alone until now because he still wasn't answering my calls. What made it even worse Brooke didn't seem to care for him or her mother when I asked where they were so I knew something was off just didn't know what.

CHAPTER 4: I SEE DEAD PEOPLE

Brooklyn/Hector

(2 months later July 2009)

Me being pregnant was starting to take a toll on me. My tolerance level for everything was getting shorter by the day. We still didn't know who was after me, and Lucas was guarding me like I was a one of a kind rare jewel that everyone wanted. I was grateful that he cared about me and my protection but looking at the same four walls was really starting to get to me. After I enrolled into Vol State Community College I pretty much cleaned the house and shopped online whenever I needed to get some things for the house.

Today I opted to swim in the pool with Nessa, Sade, Carter, Elijah, and Egypt. The sun was feeling wonderful against my skin and everyone said I had a glow that you couldn't miss. Two months ago I was a wreck when Lucas was shot and my father popped back into my life. "Hey do y'all want to go to the mall today?" I asked the girls because I needed to break free from this prison I felt like I was in.

"If Lucas lets us go then yeah," Nessa said. Sade just nodded her head. Since she found out about Zack crossing us she hasn't really spoke a word. What's worse is that she can't find him but I already knew he was somewhere swimming with the fishes.

A part of me wanted to tell her the truth but Lucas said that everything will come to light soon so I didn't stress the issue with him about it. I started to stare off into space and let my mind get the best of me. So much stuff would come across my mind lately I would zone out for at least 15 minutes at a time before I snapped back into what was going on in front of me. "Brooke snap out of it. Lucas said we could go to the mall come on," Nessa said while practically dragging me into the house to get change.

Once I got out the shower I stood in the mirror and smiled at my small baby bump that was starting to appear. Next week I was going to find out what I was having and I had gotten excited all over again. I quickly got dressed because if I stayed in this mirror any longer I wouldn't be going anywhere. I decided to throw on some grey Nike yoga pants, a black Nike shirt, and my grey Nike slide ins. It was hot outside and I wasn't in the mood to really put any clothes on.

When I went downstairs and saw that my father was in the kitchen with Lucas and Tiffany. The look the three of them gave me when I walked in let me know I was about to get a speech before I left the home. "We are sending Jigsaw and Fernando to the mall with you ladies," my father said which I already knew he was.

"Alright! That's fine with us Hector," I said which only made him mad but I didn't care. Lucas gave me a look that made me stop all my shit and get some act right quick.

"I mean that's fine with us dad," I said quickly in a much better angelic tone. When my dad shook his head and laughed I knew him and Lucas had something going on.

My father was the only person who could control me and now he was rubbing off on Lucas and I kind of liked it. "Which car are y'all taking?" Hector finally asked as I counted the cash Luc gave me.

"Can we take your Ashton Martin dad pretty please," I begged with my puppy dog eyes. When he nodded his head yes, I snatched the keys off the counter and raced out front to the car. "Don't scratch my baby up Brooklyn," he yelled front the front porch.

"Who, me or the car?" I teased because he knew not to answer that question wrong.

"Both now go have fun and don't start any shit cause your bodyguards will be right behind you," he told me and I clearly forgot they were even coming. I nodded my head and got in the car with Nessa since Sade didn't want to go with us.

"What's Sade issue now?" Nessa asked as soon as we got in the car.
"Girl at this point I don't even care. If she wants to sit around and not talk all day then let her, she not going to bring me into the deep depression with her."

"Yeah, you're right. Let's pick her up something when we get to the mall."

"I have the perfect gift in mind Nessa," I said with an evil smile.

Hector

Today I was holding a meeting to see if anyone had seen

Hector Jr. Since I had not heard from him it had my head going crazy which was the main reason I sent the girls to the mall. Sade was the only one that didn't go and it was a reason for it. I told her to stay behind because I had a few questions about Zack. I wanted to see if she had any knowledge of the plans he had going on.

When everyone arrived for the meeting I had them all sent to the basement away from the kids. Truth be told I found out last week that Egypt was mines and I was going to do everything in my power to make up for lost time. I haven't revealed it to Brooklyn yet but I'm pretty sure she's going to be fine about it. I also found out who's Carter and Elijah father was as well. They would be leaving after the meeting and I knew it was going to crush her but they wouldn't be far away.

The final guest arrived, so I placed Egypt with the nanny, the proceeded to the basement with everyone else. "Now that have everyone here. How has things been flowing lately?" I asked while going over the numbers. As everyone said there numbers I noticed that it was all correct.

"We ran into a problem last week though," Zoe my trusted Haitian said.

"With who?" I asked getting straight to the point.

"Some Mexicans looking for Oscar and Javier."

"Well what did you tell them Zoe?"

"That we haven't seen nor heard from them in months," he said quickly. Which everyone knows it's true.

I actually know Javier isn't actually dead. My people were on Javier the moment they spotted him leaving Zack's condo one night. I need to get as much information as possible from Sade to see if she knew anything about what they had going on. If she knew anything then she was going to take her last breath today and my daughter was going to hate me for this.

"Ok cool, but has anyone seen my son lately?" When I asked it was as if everyone suddenly went deaf.

"SO NOBODY HEARD WHAT I JUST ASKED," I yelled as I hit the table with my fist. Still no one said anything.

"That nigga dead. I respect you and everything you stand for but your son can burn in hell," Lucas said from the other end of the table.

I quickly grabbed my gun from my waistline and aimed it straight for his head. "Give me one good reason why I shouldn't drop you right now," I states through clenched teeth.

"Why don't you ask Brooke who landed her in the hospital the last time then boss man," he said as he got up and walked off from the table.

"Oh and by the way he's somewhere swimming with Brooke's mom too since she wanted her dead too. It looks like you've missed out on a lot and you wonder why Brooke hated you when you first came back. You could've prevented all of this but you only worry about yourself Hector," he said then exited the room.

As much as I wanted to put a bullet in his ass he was right. I only cared about myself and no one else at times. Yes, I was very selfish and that almost caused my daughter her life twice. I now see it's time for me to focus more on my family, than I did my money. It seems like we had a lot of family issues I needed to discuss. I just pray it isn't too late.

"You're all dismissed. Call Brooke and tell her when she gets here we need to have a talk. I need Javier picked back up, and also brings Zack ass with him it's time for some skeletons to come out of the closet," I order Larry my right hand man to do. When I snapped my finger he was off just like that.

"Send Sade in too" I ordered.
See this is the shit that makes me feel like a failure. Hell truth be told I am a failure but only as a father. I've always been successful in life at everything but being a father. If I would have stayed around this shit would have been handled years ago. I needed to put my foot down again and it was about to be hell for everyone that crossed me while I was gone no matter who you were.

When Sade walked in the room I read her energy that quick. I still needed to make sure I was making the right decision. "Did you know about Zack crossing us?" I asked her when she sat down at the table.

"No," she said as she looked me in my eyes with tears starting to form. At this point she thought she knew his faith but he wasn't dead yet.

"Alright you can go now," I told her as I lit the cigar in my hand and made my way towards the door.

"Is he dead?" She asked as soon as I reached the door.

"You will find out sooner or later," I told her as I left the room.

If she didn't have anything to do with it she could live, but if she was then she was putting on a hell of a front but truth me when I say I will find out if she's lying or not. He phone has been tapped, along with her social media, her car, her home, and Zack's places as well. It's time for me to step back in head first with full force. Being away had me blind to a lot of shit lately but not anymore.

CHAPTER 5: I WANT OUT
Brooklyn

The moment I stepped in the mall I felt like shit was off. I hating having this feeling and something was telling me to go back home but I was tired of being in the house. Honestly being pregnant had my hormones and feelings all over the place so I'm probably tripping for nothing, plus Fernando and Jigsaw was with us anyway and Jigsaw didn't let shit slip past him.

The first place we went to was the food court because I was starving. "Nessa what you want to eat I'm hungry," I asked while looking at all the places trying to decide on what to eat from there.

"Nothing here lets grab food by the house when we leave from here. I hate to say it but she don't feel right," she finally said and I knew I wasn't tripping then.

"What's wrong with y'all," Jigsaw asked us while looking around the food court.

"Shit don't feel right man. We're just going to shop and get out of here," I said while walking towards Bath & Body Works.

"You sure. I mean we got y'all back, but if you want to go sit in the car I'll get all the stuff while y'all wait with Fernando," he said.

"Naw, we're good just watch us closely and don't let us out of your sight. If the feeling I'm feeling is right let's bait the fish," I told him while grabbing a bag to shop.

"How you want to do this then boss?" Fernando asked while looking around to make sure we weren't being watched.

"Y'all go out the back door and stay there it's a cut right by Journeys that will lead us to y'all so the second whoever it is sees us by ourself I'm sure they will follow us right into to y'all," I said while walking through the store grabbing all of my favorite sets.

Once I made sure I had everything I made my way to the register with Nessa just as the boys left out through the back door. "Your total is $328.46," the cashier said which snapped me out of my thoughts. When I paid I looked over at Nessa who was so into her phone she didn't even see Marcus walk up behind her.

"Y'all good sis? Lucas sent me to check on y'all to make sure y'all was good," Marcus said while eyeing Nessa. I think he really came just to see what she was doing and snatch her away.

"We good, I just think some shit trying to pop off but I could be wrong," I told him.

"I see y'all set a trap since Fernando and Jigsaw are missing,"

Marcus said while looking around.

"Yup, so take Nessa and stay a few feet behind me," I told him.

When I finally made my way out of the store I was alone and no longer worried to do anything stupid. I never feared jail, I just didn't want Nessa getting caught up in the shit that I do because jail was not for her. I'm a fighter and Nessa is more of a lover. She could handle her own but in jail I knew if they separated us then everything would go downhill for her. I pray she stayed far away if my intuition was right.

When I walked out the store the feeling only got worse. The second I hit the corner I noticed someone hot on my tail. I couldn't make out who the person was and I hoped it was just me jumping to my conclusions like I normally do. I stopped by the bathrooms just to make sure I wasn't going crazy. I checked my clothes in the mirror then proceeded to head back out the bathroom to the hallway.

"Someone is following you. I'm a friend of your fathers come with me," the mystery lady told me. When we exit the bathroom we hit the double doors to the left then went through another set and I saw Jigsaw, Fernando, Nessa, Marcus, and about 40 other goons with them. I looked around and figured that shit could only be worser then what I expected.

"Take the tunnel to the right it goes underground and also you will be undetected as well. Follow it until you see the black trucks and they will lead you home. Lucas has already picked the cars up from here," the lady to me. One thing I noticed she was a bad bitch and fine as hell though.

"Who are you?" I finally asked because I was tired of all the secrets.

"I'm your real mother Brooke. Everything will be explained when we get back to the house now go," she demanded me and just like that I took my ass into the tunnels with everyone else so that we could get going.

The more I sat back and wondered what else I was being lied to about the more I put shit together on how the woman who I thought was my mom treated me the way that she did. I had so many answers and as bad as I wanted them they will have to wait. "So did y'all know who my mom really was or what," I finally asked breaking the silence as we headed towards the exit in the tunnel. No one said anything so to keep from going off I had to bite down on my inner jaw because my mouth could get real reckless. If Lucas knew about this, he better hope that god could help him from the wrath he was going to feel.

Once we finally reached the end of the tunnel there was a heard of black trucks. "Oh you look just like your mother," and older lady said getting out the back of one of the many trucks. I quickly snatched away from her because I didn't know who the hell she was and I didn't like for people to touch my face.

"Don't touch my fucking face! Who the fuck are you anyway?" I asked hoping I got a few answers from her.

"A mouth and attitude like your mothers, get in the car Brooklyn now is not the time for questions," she told me.

"I will ask whatever the fuck I want to ask. Now like I said who the hell are you because I don't get in the car with strangers you old hag," I finally told her.

"Brooke that's your grandmother get your stubborn ass in the fucking truck now," I heard my father yell from behind me.

"Hector you can kiss my ass with all the bullshit I keep finding out, as a matter of fact I'll go home when I fucking feel like it,"

I told him as I snatched the keys from the driver and drove off.

The calls from my dad were coming back to back so I quickly turned my phone off because I didn't have time to listen to any of his lies. Between the tears and my clouded mind I could hardly focus on driving. To say that I was upset was an understatement but the family I thought I had was no longer my family. My life was based off lies and I wanted so bad to know why but knowing my dad I would never get the truth.

My ringing phone snapped me out of my thoughts. I quickly forgot all about the other phone I had which I knew it could only be one person. When I pulled it out of my Louis Vuitton crossover I looked at the screen and saw Lucas name appear. I wanted to answer it but I already knew he was probably near my father so I wasn't going to.

My hour drive quickly turned into 4 hours before I decided to head to Lucas condo that he hardly ever went to. When I pulled into the garage I didn't see anyone's cars or trucks in there so I knew the coast was clear for me to head up. I quickly made my way to the top floor by taking the stairs. I knew I was going to regret this but right now I didn't care.

When I peeped from the door to the stairwell and didn't see anybody guards by the door I made my way over to unlock it. I went into the kitchen and grabbed my set of keys and quickly left before anyone came here looking for me. I went down to the 15th floor and went into my condo that my uncle purchased for me that I hadn't used in years.

When I walked inside I could tell the maid service still came to clean it and keep food in it every two weeks. I went into my bedroom and opened the curtains that looked over the city. It was night time and the night skies looked so good. My bathroom windows were the same way so I went into it to start my bath water. I always knew my dad lied to me a lot but I never would've thought he would fake his death and also have a bitch who isn't my mother raise me. The more I thought about it the more the shit pissed me off.

Once my bath water was ran I lit a few candles and dimmed the lights in the bathroom. I loved darkness and the setting right now was relaxing to me. The only light I had was the few candles, the city lights, and the dim lights. A part of me wish Lucas was here but I really didn't want to be around my family right now. I felt like I no longer had a family.

It was going on 8:45pm when I had finally gotten out of the tub. I rubbed myself down in some coco butter and baby oil gel because my skin felt so dry. I grabbed my robe then made my way towards the living room before I stopped and looked at myself in front of the mirror. The look in my eyes was something of a lost lonely child. The bags under my eyes showed lack of sleep because the baby was starting to keep me up every night due to the fact that I couldn't keep anything down anymore. My round belly was the only thing that made me feel complete. It was the little movement inside of me that snapped me back to reality.

When I went into the kitchen I grabbed some chicken and turned the deep fryer on. The only reason I was eating was because of the baby. I didn't have an appetite but I needed to eat so my baby boy or girl could grow big and strong. I grabbed some green beans, corn, mashed potatoes, and rolls to go along with my chicken. After about an hour I was sitting down stuffing my face as if it were no tomorrow.

After I finished eating I cleaned the kitchen and returned to my bed for the night. I was so sleepy that I didn't even hear my phone going off for the 30th time until it hit the floor. I woke up cause the sound of it crashing sounded like someone was breaking into my condo. I looked and noticed it was still Lucas calling so I decided to answer it. "Hello", I said in a sleepy tone.

"Are you ok?" Lucas asked.

"Yes I'm fine. I'm in the bed." I told him.

"Okay," was all he said before he ended the line. When I looked at the clock I noticed it was 2am so I rolled back over and went right back to sleep.

CHAPTER 6: YOU'RE NEVER ALONE

Lucas

The second I found out about Brooke's real mother I knew she was going to need her space for a few. With her being pregnant her hormones were everywhere so I played like I didn't know where she would go when Hector asked me. It was going on 2am and I had finally left his house and I was headed to her condo downtown. Javier brought it for her when she kept getting put out but she ever used it because she hated being alone because she always felt like she was being watched.

When I entered the smell of her cooking hit my nose so I went straight to the kitchen to get me a plate. To my surprise it was in the microwave so she must've known I was going to find her. I grabbed a water out of the fridge then sat at the bar to eat. Once I finished I took my shoes off and made my way to our room. She was sleeping so peacefully I almost didn't want to wake her but I missed my lady and just wanted to make sure she was ok.

I went into the bathroom to take a shower because I hated to go to bed with dirt anywhere on me. After about 45 minutes I was drying off and brushing my teeth. Once I finished I climbed in bed and she still didn't move. I knew she was tired but I just had to wake her. I shook her gently in her sleep and she jumped out of the bed with her gun in her hand.

"Shit, Lucas you scared the fuck out of me," she told me. I took the gun from her and put it down.

"I'm sorry baby. I knew you would be here so I came over once your father finally let everyone go. I know you have a lot on your mind but I'm not going to let you sleep alone," I said while pulling her into my arms.

It's like I felt her stress leave her body once I grabbed, and held onto her. I wish I could just disappear with her but I knew I couldn't just yet. There were still answers we needed and she needed them fast. When I felt her tears hit my chest my anger hit an all-time high.

"Baby stop all that crying you're too pretty for that. The stressing you're doing isn't good for the baby either so chill, everything is going to be ok," I told her while rubbing her back.

"I'm not crying because of my dad. I'm crying because my stomachs hurts Lucas," she said sounding offended.

"Come on you're going to the hospital then," I told her while practically dragging her out of the bed to get dressed.

About five minutes later we were leaving out the front door. It only took us about 10 minutes to get to the hospital since we were already downtown. The second I stepped into Centennial Woman's Hospital I was yelling for help. Finally a nurse heard me and came running right to us because at this point Brooke could hardly walk. "What's wrong with her?" the nurse asked as soon as we put Brooke into a wheelchair.

"She started crying and said her stomach was hurting so to be honest I'm not too sure wats going on," I told the nurse because Brooke was now screaming and could hardly talk.

When we got into a room I helped the nurse put Brooke onto the bed so that she could see if she was in early labor. Once we undressed her the lady laid the bed down flat. "Ok Brooke you're going to feel some pressure I'm just checking your cervix ok love," the nurse told her.

It took all of 10 seconds for her to check Brooke and the nurse finally said, "She's not in labor. What did she eat today?"

"Well she had fried chicken, green beans, mashed potatoes, corn, and some rolls," I told the nurse.

"Well let's get a ultrasound done so when can see what's going on with the baby. He or she might be in a position that's hurting her," she told me.

When the nurse left the room, I turned back to Brooke who seemed to have calmed down but was still in pain. "Are you still in pain?" I asked as soon as she looked up at me.

"Yes, I'm just trying to bear with it for now," she said.

"I'm right here for you no matter what. I love you and our unborn and will love the both of you until the day I take my last breath," I told her while kissing her forehead and rubbing her cheek.

I grabbed the chair next to her bed and scooted it over to

her bed. Just then the nurse came back into the room with a machine. She but some clear jelly on her stomach then took the bob in her hand and place it on her stomach and moved it around. When the baby appeared on the screen and was moving around I finally stopped holding my breath because I started thinking the worst. "Well it looks like she was sitting on a nerve so you should be fine once she moves completely off of it," the nurse told her.

"She? It's a girl?" Brooke asked.

"Yes ma'am you all will be having a girl," she confirmed.

I wanted my first child to be a boy but that fact that I was having a girl first means I had to go even harder in the streets to make my exit soon. Brooklyn was clearly excited because she was shedding tears at the fact that she was going to have a mini me. I whipped the tears from her eyes and gave her the most passionate kiss ever. If she wasn't already pregnant she surly would've been after tonight.

When the pain finally went away the nurse gave us her discharge papers and we were heading home. It was going on 7am and I really needed to get some sleep and so did she. We went back to the condo because she wasn't ready to face her father or her real mother right now, but what she didn't know was that she was meeting them later on today rather she wanted to or not. When we got to the condo I ran our bath water, put lavender crystals, and lavender bubble bath in it so she could relax a little better.

I undressed her and helped her into the water. Once I made sure she was ok I went and got her some water and fruit before I got into join her. I slid in the tub behind her and turned the jets on to the tub. The only reason I liked this condo was because of the view of the city and the jacuzzi tub. She always thought she could keep stuff from me but she knew she couldn't. I find out everything without even trying.

I wanted to ask her about the situation with her mother and father but I wanted to wait until she was well relaxed for it. Since she's been pregnant her hormones and attitude have been all over the place. My job was to make her life peaceful not add to the stress. I grabbed her loaf and began to wash her back while she washed her legs with her washcloth. Once we washed her entire body twice I washed up then turned the shower on so that we could wash up again. I had a thing about dirt and when taking a bath you sit in your own dirt so I always shower after my bath.

Once we were dried off and put lotion on I pulled the covers back on the bed and helped her climb right into it. She didn't really like the heat so she was sleeping naked like she has been doing lately. The moment I heard her light snores I grabbed my phone to send my mother a text before I passed out myself.

Me: Ma were at the condo took Brooke to the ER last night just now getting in. You know which one we're in so grab some food and come over. Get the key out of my condo to let yourself in. Bring the kids and don't tell anyone where you're going.

Ma: Is she okay? Alright son. We probably won't be there until later on. Get some sleep.

Me: Yes the baby was sitting on her nerve she's finally sleeping now. Oh and by the way it's a girl.

Ma: congratulations son I'm happy for the both of you. Now rest up we will be there later one to cook.

Me: Ok ma. I love you.

Ma: I love you too son.

I put my phone on the nightstand and grabbed the remote that controlled the shades in the house. I pulled down the black shades so that it would be darker for us then laid there just thinking about what the future held. I didn't know anything about raising a daughter but I'm sure it wouldn't be too hard. One thing my daughter was going to know was the game that some of these little boys liked to play. There was no way I was letting any nigga get over on my baby girl unless you wanted me to burry you 8ft deep with acid on top your body. I had no problem making someone disappear for my loved ones.

I really couldn't sleep because I didn't want to sleep to hard and Brooke started having pain again. Instead I went into the living room with my laptop and started looking for themes for the baby nursery. I found a few I liked so instead of asking Brooklyn I started ordering things and opted for same day delivery. By the time she woke up the condo was going to be totally different but in a good way.

The extra room was empty so when the painters got there first they started putting plastic down over the hardwood floors so that they wouldn't mess them up. I went with pink and purple and also got some glitter to throw on the wall as well. Two of the walls were pink with purple stripes and glitter. While the other two walls were purple with pink stripes and glitter. When I was done with this room Brooklyn would love it.

I let the paint dry while I waited for the furniture to be delivered. I went into the room to find my baby was still knocked out. I probably stood there for a good 30 minutes before I heard the door buzzer going off. It took the delivery men all of 45 minutes to put the furniture together and once they finished I locked the condo back up then headed to take a nap with my baby. The second I laid in the bed my phone started ringing. I was about to answer it until my baby said, "Baby turn your phone off or put it on silent I really don't want to be alone today."

Without saying anything I powered my phone off and put it

on the nightstand.

"You know that as long as I have air in my lungs you will never be alone," I told her as she lay in my arms with her hand on my chest.

"I know baby, but since I found out about my family I just feel like I have no one," she said. I sat up in the bed and she sat up right next to me.

I looked her in the eyes and told her, "I love you and our daughter y'all will never be alone. Now go back to sleep because I'm tired and you need your rest," I told her.

"I love you and our daughter too," she told me then gave me a kiss and laid back down.

The second my head hit the pillow I was out. I probably had been up for longer than 24 hours and I really needed some sleep. I hated the fact that Brooklyn was feeling all alone. I mean I know she only meant family wise but I'm her family now and she should never feel alone. I need to plan a quick getaway so she can get her mind together because once the baby gets here we won't be going anywhere for a while.

My mind was going heavy and before I knew it I was back up. The way she felt did something to me and I refused to let her feel this way any longer. Right then I knew what I had to do. I sent a text to her father, Nessa, Sade, Marcus, Ricky, and Poppy on where to meet me tomorrow. My mom was coming over so I would tell her when she got here. When everything was finished it was going on 3pm so I laid down to finally take a nap.

I was awaken by the smell of food and just knew my mom and Brooklyn were in the kitchen cutting up. I made my way into the bathroom to relieve myself of the fluids that had built up in my bladder. Then, I brushed my teeth and washed my face. When I walked out of the room I went into the kitchen to find Brooke and my mother looking at baby girl room decorations. Little did they know they were in for a surprise. "What are my two lovely ladies over there doing?" I asked as I looked on the stove to see what they were cooking.

"Looking at baby décor son. Are you well rested now?"

"Yeah I'm good ma," I said. I went into the fridge to grab a bottle of water then sat at the bar next to Brooke.

I looked at all the pages she had marked and new I did my job just right. "I have a surprise for you," I told her.

"What is it baby," she asked.

"Come on I'll show you," I told her as I took her hand and lead her to the baby nursery. When I opened the door to she room she screamed with joy.

"Baby I love it," she told me while jumping up and down.

"Good now let's eat I'm hungry as hell," I told her as I made my way back into the kitchen.

When we got back in the kitchen I started to fix Brooklyn plate till she yelled at me and said, "Boy move I got your plate."
"Girl this your plate, and you need your rest go sit your ass down over there," I told her while pointing to the bar in the kitchen. When I sat her plate down in front of her she turned her nose up at me.

"What girl?"

"Why you put this much food on my plate Lucas?"

"Girl you eating for two feed my daughter before I feed her for you," I told her while laughing. She rolled her eyes at me and started eating.

The fried chicken is always my favorite along with the macaroni and cheese. My mom also made some turnip greens, corn bread, and a pound cake for desert. The food was so good nobody in the house was even talking. Once we were doing eating I cleaned the kitchen while my mom and Brooke talked and of course I was ease dropping. The more she opened up to my mom the more my decision about tomorrow was making more sense to me. After tomorrow that shit she was feeling was going out the window rather she liked it or not.

By the time I finished cleaning the kitchen Brooklyn was sleep so I brought my mom up to speed on what I was doing tomorrow and she was all for it. Once she left I turned the alarm on then went into the bedroom to grab my phone. I sat on the balcony smoking a fat blunt while responding to a few messages.

I noticed it was going on midnight so I retreated to the shower. I crawled in the bed at 1am and spooned Brooke. When I rubbed her belly the baby kicked back and I couldn't help but leave my hand there. Everywhere I moved my hand she followed. She was a daddy's girl already and I was ready for the last few months to fly by. I kissed her belly and told the baby I love her, then I did the same to Brooklyn.

CHAPTER 7: A DREAM COME TRUE

Brooklyn

Last night I opened up to Lucas mom more and I just felt like she understood everything that I felt right now. It didn't take long for me to get tired when I finished eating so the second I take a shower I crashed when I hit the bed. I looked over to Lucas and he was still asleep. I fixed him breakfast and took it into the room on a tray. When he finally woke up he was smiling and ready to eat.

Right after we finished breakfast we headed to the shower

to get our day started. For some reason my hormones were on 10 and I really needed him beating my walls down right now. I looked up at him and watched him get undressed while biting on my bottom lip.

"Daddy I need some dick like now," I told him. When he turned around showing that evil as a smile I couldn't do anything but laugh at him.

"Let daddy taste," he told me while leading me into the shower.

I stood under the shower while his hands roamed my body knowing all my spots to touch and how to touch them. When his lips touched my neck I almost climaxed. He pushed my head back and let his tongue find its way to my nipple. The way he sucked and nibbled on them cause me to let out a small moan as his hand massaged my pearl. "That's the spot baby," I moaned to him.

The second he took his tongue and played it on my pearl I had to grab the back of his head to keep from falling. He liced on my like a cat licking milk from a bowl and within seconds I was climaxing all over his face and he loved it. I tried to push his face away from my pearl but he wouldn't let go. Not even 3 minutes later I was coming again and his beard was soaked. He sat down on the bent and motioned me to take my seat on my thrown.

As much as we had sex it still hurt every time the head went in. "Fuck," I moaned as I finally had him inside of me. The way I went up and down on his shaft had me going into overdrive. My juices were leaking and he was loving every bit of it. "Damn baby slow down," he told me and I wasn't trying to hear it. The way he almost had me crying he was about to get this work rather he liked it or not.

The echoes of my ass smacking against his lap as I was riding him was turning me on and I was climaxing again. I sped up the paste and seconds later he was coming and screaming FUCK to the top of his lungs. I thought I was being extra but clearly he wasn't.

"Bend over," he told me when I got off his lap. The back shots he delivered to me were deadly because I was trying my best to run out that shower but he was not letting me go.

He slide in and out of me fast and hard. I was climaxing back to back and my legs got weak which almost caused me to fall. His deep stroke had my hormones going crazier and I couldn't help but screw, out his name. "Fuck Lucas. Go harder. Right there. Don't stop," I told him as I started to throw it back on him.

He held on to the shower wall at that point to keep his balance so neither one of us would slip and fall. The second I started to slow down he told me, "What you doing baby. Ain't no slowing down you been begging for it so take yo dick."

I turned to look at him and started to laugh cause he was always saying silly shit. "Baby I'm tired and my legs are weak. Can we just stop and take a nap now," I asked him.

"No nap we got things to do so wash up," he said while sliding out of me and smacking my ass. I jumped a little because it stung.

We washed up twice then got out of the shower. We both brushed our teeth, flossed, and washed our face. Once we lotioned our body down I put on my bath robe then went into my closet to find something to wear. It was July and very hot out so I opted for my white denim shorts with a white cut off sleeve shirt by Dior. I pulled out my white and gold Dior sandals and slide my feet right into them. I grabbed my necklace that spelled LUCAS and grabbed my L snapped diamond earrings and put them on. My hair was bone straight and I was loving it because it was down to my ass. Did I mention it was my real hair too.

I saw Lucas roaming around in his closet when I went back into mines to grab my diamond tennis bracelet. Once I exited my closet I sat on the bed to wait until Lucas was ready. By the time he came out fully dressed and in all white as will I had fallen asleep. "Baby come on we have to get going," he told me as she lightly shook me out of my sleep. I grabbed the book *Moth To A Flame* off my book shelf and followed Lucas to the parking garage. We got into his all white Range Rover and headed towards the strip downtown.

We meet one of his buyers at Joe's Crab Shack and I was dying for some seafood. When we were seated in the upstairs seating area on the balcony, I quickly ordered me a water with extra ice. Lucas order a double short of Parton. Once the waiter brought us our drinks we order our food because I was ready to eat and this girl had me starving. I ordered a pound of the Peel N Eat Shrimp, a bucket of Snow Crabs, and the Joe's Classic Steam pot. Lucas looked at me and shook his head. He only ordered Snow Crabs.

"That's all you're going to eat," I asked him as I looked into his eyes.

"Baby you ordered enough for both of us. I'll eat whatever you don't eat," he told me.

"What about me for desert," I asked as I bit on my bottom lip.

"How about now in the bathroom then," he said and I was more than ready.

"You to love birds can do that later we have work to first," said Franky his Italian buyer who always spent major with us. I stood up to give Franky a hug then he slapped hands with Lucas.

The meeting ending quickly and he told us he would see us later on. While we enjoyed our lunch, I noticed his phone was ringing nonstop and I'm sure it was no one but my father. I looked and him and he passed me his phone. I answered and told him, "I have nothing to say to you right now," then ended the call. I guess he got the picture because he didn't call back.

"Baby you know I'm not trying to tell you what to do, but you need to hear him out. You only get one mother and one father. Once they're gone it ain't no coming back. So call him back and tell him you will see him later on," he told and I did it as a tear slid down my cheek.

He always had a way of making me feel so bad when I felt like I wasn't doing anything wrong. One thing about me is that I had a bad temper and was use to getting my way, but lately he's been making me do a complete 360. I dried my face and just looked at him with the I hate you but I love you too face at the same time. "I understand that you're hurt but you will thank me later," he told me.

"If you say so, but what are we doing today anyway," I asked.

"You will see, let's go," he said.

When he paid, we got back into the car and headed over to a church where one of his other buyers preachers at. "Come on because this meeting might take a while," he said. I really didn't want to go in but I didn't have a choice so I got my ass out the seat and went inside.

"Are you ready?"

I looked at him confused and asked," Ready for what?"

"To officially take my last name?" I looked at him in shock because I thought he was playing but he was clearly serious.

Once inside I realized that he wasn't. I found my mother, my father, my friends, and pretty much all of my loved ones inside waiting for us.

"You can plan the real wedding after this but I didn't want another day to go by without you being my wife," he said as he looked me in the eyes and I begin to cry like a baby.

"You ready to become Mrs. Lucas Jenkins?"

"Been ready since I was 15," I told him which everyone knew that was true.

Thirty minutes later I was walking out of the church as Mrs. Brooklyn Taylor Jenkins. One thing about us is that you could clearly see the happiness and love we had for each other. I felt like I was on a cloud everyday with him. No matter if I was mad or sad I always felt the love for him and from him no matter what terms we were on.

"Mrs. Jenkins what do you want to do right now," he asked.

"Baby I just want to take a nap because your daughter is on 10 right now," I said while rubbing my belly.

"How about this I'll take you home to take a nap, I'll go make a few drops then we can head out after that. How does that sound?"

"Like a plan baby but if I'm sleep don't wake me just carry my spoiled ass up to the room ok?" He knew I was serious because he started laughing and shaking his head yes.

In reality I wanted to do something special for him but of course after my nap. Just like I knew I would I fell asleep the moment we got in the car. When we pulled up at home I stayed sleep because I really didn't want to walk. He carried me in bridal style and I was loving every moment of it. I had my phone in my hand so I snapped a picture before we got to the front door. I never would've thought I'd be married to this man but here I am and I'm happy as hell that it finally happened too.

I let him put me in bed, undress me, and put me under the covers. He even turned the fan on and shut the blinds so that the sun wouldn't wake me up. He kissed me on my forehead, then my belly and told me that he loved me. I had to stop myself from saying it back since I was suppose to be sleep. The moment he left, and I heard the front door close and lock, I quickly jumped out the bed and got dressed. I waited a good 20 minutes before I left the house because he sometimes liked to double back if he forgot something.

I got on the elevator and headed down to the garage. I quickly called up Nessa to see if she was busy and of course she wasn't.

"Nessa you want to ride with me real quick," I asked her the second she answered the phone.

"Yea, I'm at Marcus house he left to go with Lucas and I'm bored so hurry up," she told me.

"Okay I'll be there in 10 minutes and don't tell Marcus you going with me. I'm suppose to be sleep but I need to get Lucas a gift first," I told her.

"Girl you know I won't now hurry up I bored and hungry bitch," she told me.

When I got in the car, I quickly backed up and pulled out the garage. It took me 8 minutes to get to Marcus house and I blew the horn and she came running out. "What do you have in mind for his present?"

"To be honest Nessa I don't know. He always said he wanted a Ferrari so let's see what strings I can pull," I told her as I hoped on the interstate and headed to the dealership in Franklin.

On the ride out we caught up on a lot since I disappeared after finding out about my real mom the other day. "Have you talked to them yet?"

"No not yet. I can't really face them because I was lied to and almost died twice. I mean all this shit could've been avoided if my real mother would've raised me on her own," I told Nessa.

"True I understand but at least talk to them. Not a day goes by that I don't miss my mom. I wish we ended on better terms but that's neither here nor there. Yours is still alive so make it right while you can," she expressed to me.

"I will just not right now maybe after we do this I will stop by and talk to them," I said.

Just as we pulled into the dealership I saw the perfect car to get him. I ended up getting him a 2010 corvette coupe ZR1 with 638 horsepower. One thing about Lucas was that he loved his cars so it was only right I got him this since I couldn't find a Ferrari. Nessa followed me back to the condo so we could put the car up then head to my dad's house. I would've drove Lucas new car over there but I decided to just go in the black G Wagon instead.

The ride to my father's house was silent. My mind was racing and I didn't really know what to think right now. I hope I didn't get a bullshit answer because if I did I knew my mouth was going to have me in trouble. When I pulled up to the home I grew up in before my father faked his death it was as if nothing had changed.

I used my key to let me and Nessa in and went straight to my old room. Nothing had been touched and it looked as if someone keep it clean cause it was not any dust in sight. I came across some pictures of us in middle school and I couldn't help but to laugh at how we looked back then. "Have you seen or heard from Sade," I asked Nessa as I looked at a picture of all three of us together in high school during our freshmen year.

"No not since the day we went to the mall and found out about your mom," she replied to me.

"Oh, okay! Let's go find Hector and this woman who claims she's my mom. I'm sure she's around here somewhere," I spat while walking out of my old room.

We made our way to the kitchen were someone had cooked not sure who but the food smelled too damn good to just let it sit there and go to waste. I fixed me a plate of backed chicken, sweet potatoes, macaroni and cheese, turnip greens, white rice, and rolls. I heard noises coming from downstairs so I opted to eat in the kitchen before I made my way down there. Once we finished eating we headed to the basement.
Long and be hold I found my dad and my mom having sex. When I say he had her bent, home Girl was bent all the way over. I couldn't do shit but laugh. "Damn daddy you keep hitting her like that and she gone run out of my life again," I said. They both jumped up while he and Nessa laughed at them.

"Don't you know how to knock on the fucking door," my dad yelled at me.

"Chill Hector I still have my key. Who cook that food because it was pretty good," I asked while eating another roll.

"Your mother did, and we need to talk. Talk y'all ass upstairs so we can get dressed," he told us.

"Nigga we not even looking at y'all, I'm trying to figure out when the hell you get a swimming pool put in down here," I said walking past them.

Growing up seeing naked people never bothered me. I will see a family member naked and walk right past them as if they didn't exist. "It was put in last year. Javier had it put in," he told me.

"Awe, we'll be upstairs waiting for y'all to love birds. Um one more thing dad where's Tiffany," I asked.

"So you still fucking with that rat face bitch Tiffany huh," my mom yelled while hitting my dad in the jaw. Me and Nessa started laughing and quickly went upstairs.

The last thing I heard was my dad saying, "Brooklyn I'm going to beat your ass" before I was hit in the back of the head with a gun and blacked out.

CHAPTER 8: THERE'S A SNAKE IN THE GRASS

Hector

When Brooklyn found out about her real mother I cursed myself for not telling her sooner because I knew how she was going to react. The fact that she just burst in the house while I was fucking her mom's brains out irritated me. What pissed me off was that she asked about Tiffany and her mother hated Tiffany. See the real reason behind me faking my death was because I was on the feds radar and the family was not getting along. Tiffany was an old hoe from back in the day that did whatever I told her to do and never asked me any questions.

I loved Brooklyn's mother dearly but she always got under my skin. Truth is me and Brooklyn's real mother are actually married. When I found out what happened at the mall I quickly sent Tiffany back to Jamaica and told her I'll be there in a few months to not contact me for anything. Truth was I wasn't going to hit her up but she was going to come up missing. But the fact that Brooklyn told her mom about it made me furious. "So you still fucking with that bitch huh? You know what nigga, kiss my ass and go to hell," she yelled at me.

"Bae just chill man. It's not even like that. She been cut off. I didn't know when you were coming back so yeah I was just fucking the bitch that's it. Last time I checked I was married to you, I love you not her so chill that fucking noise and keep your got damn hands to your fucking self," I barked her.

She rolled her eyes and grabbed her robe off the couch then headed upstairs. I grabbed my pants, slid my shoes on, and grabbed my gun and went up right behind her. When I got upstairs I didn't see Brooklyn or Nessa anywhere. "Bee you see the girls?"

"No go check her room," she demanded me and guess what I did? Walked my ass out that kitchen.

"Yo, why the fuck the front door wide open," I yelled.

"I don't know," she barked back as I went running past her back to the kitchen.

"FFFFFFUUUCK!!!!!! Get dressed now Javier took her," I yelled.

I went back into the basement and brought up a case that has been under my bed for years. Today was the day that all this beef shit ended. Today was the day the lies stopped and the truth finally came out. "Javier has Brooklyn and Nessa get Marcus and the crew and meet me at the warehouse now," I demanded Lucas the second he answered his phone.

"Hector I don't mean no disrespect but if anything happens to her or our daughter I promise you somebody gone feel my wrath," he spat then ended the line.

Bee and I both dressed in all black and headed to the garage.

I put the case I had and put it into the trunk of the truck and headed to the shelf in the garage. I grabbed a bullet proof vest along with extra ammunition. "Hector please don't let anything happen to our baby girl or our granddaughter," Bee told me while shedding tears.

"Bella nothing will happen to her or the baby. We have the best people in the team including us looking for her. No stone will go untouched. Do you still have that connect with the FBI and Metro?"

"Now you know I do," she told me.

"Make that call, we will need the backup. Are sure they will keep it off the radar since we have extra people with us just in case bodies drop," I told her while kissing her cheek.

"I got you daddy," she said then we hopped in the car and sped off.

The ride to the warehouse was a quiet one. I'm not sure if Bella hated me or loved me right now. It's like something is always happening to our baby girl and I'm sick of it. I was suppose to keep her safe no matter how old she was and I was failing very hard right now. In the past few years she's been near death so many times I pray this was the last time that it actually happens to her because this time shit was going to end bad for whoever had something to do with it. She is suppose to die after me not before me.

When we pulled into the warehouse everyone had already beat us there even the FBI and Metro. I mean we did pay them well whenever we called so I was use to that. "Hector, Bella long time no see," Agent Foster said.

"Ricky Foster, how's the family," I asked.

"Not too good. Angie left with the kids. Fuck am I saying life's great I miss my kids but not their mother," he joked.

"She's still a bitch I see," I told him.

"You look in the dictionary you'll see her picture right next to bitch," he said and everyone started to laugh.

What a lot of people also didn't know was Jigsaw was my son. I never knew how he was living because I never knew about him until I came back to town. The second I walked in the warehouse I knew exactly who he was. Bella was going to hate me for this one but right now I needed to air all my dirty laundry to the team. Once the last piece to the puzzle finally arrived I knew then that I could begin.

"Now that everyone is here it's time I bring you all up to speed with my family drama. Nessa and Brooklyn were taking from my house by Javier, Zack, and Sade. You see the house they were taken from only a few people knew about it. As far as the people in this room only which is Lucas, Marcus, Ricky, Bella, and myself knew about it. Which means one of us had to tip them off that they were at my house," I said calmly.

"What the fuck was she doing at your house anyway. I took her home and she was suppose to had been sleeping until I got back there. So as far as her being at your house I had no clue because her ass was supposed to been at home sleep cause she damn sure was sleep when I left," Lucas told me. I knew he was upset hell his wife was missing and on top of that she was pregnant. I felt the pain in his voice and I couldn't wait to find her cause if he was anything like his father which I knew he was, he could be very deadly when pissed completely off.

"I'm not sure. I called her and told her I wanted to talk and she sounds like she was out to me cause I heard the wind in the background," I told him.

When he pinched the bridge of his nose like his father I knew shit was about to go left and very quick. "Where's the I.T. guy I know how we can find her we don't have time for the family drama shit right now," he said calmly.

"Right here," Brian said. He was the quiet one in the group. I was mad that I took him off my payroll when I faked my death but I wish I would have kept him on Brooklyn and Javier cause none of this shit would have happened.

"What type of tracker do you have on her?" Brian asked.

"That's for me to know and for y'all to never find out. Just give me your laptop. I don't trust anyone in this room right now especially you pigs," he said.

"Lucas chill that's not called for right now," I told him.

"I'll chill when my wife and unborn daughter are back in fucking sight. I'll just use my phone y'all better be able to keep up with my speed on the highway," he barked.

Lucas

When Hector called and told me Brooklyn had been taken I lost it. Every time some shit pops off I think it's because of me but it goes back to Hector and his fucking skeletons in his closet that

I FELL IN LOVE WITH THE PLUG 3

he has. When he tried to spill his dirt I told him we didn't have time. See I have a tracker on Brooklyn, just as she has one on me but nobody knows. It's more of a security thing for the both of us if something like this is to happen. My dad had one on my mom, my brothers, me, and his self so of course it was only right I did the same with my family.

I'm usually the one that keeps quite not wanting to show my dark side but from the looks of it Brooklyn was also about to see a side of me she never knew. When I say nobody was off limits when it came to my family nobody was. Not even her friends. I should have put a bullet in Sade when I had the chance but I didn't. It seemed funny the way she ran out the house that day Hector asked her about Zack crossing us. She claimed she didn't know but I had a feeling that she knew because since that day no one has seen nor heard from her.

When I activated her gps I got a signle and it was pinging off of a building off of an old dirt road in the country, when I say country I mean the country. "I hope everyone is on full cause it looks like we're headed to Cross Plains, Tennessee," I told everyone.

"The hell are they doing all the way out there?" Jigsaw questioned?

"Ask he mother and father because from the looks on their faces it looks as if they know," I stated as I walked towards my truck. Once everyone was in their rides we headed out to go get my wife and unborn.

The entire ride there I silently cried and prayed. I wasn't a man that prayed a lot but I had a lot to pray about today. I also wasn't a man that cried but I can't live without Brooklyn. Here I am crying over her when I didn't even cry at my own father's funeral. After we arrived we all went out into a field where no one could see us from because the grass was so high. "Hey Brian do you have that program where you can see how many people are in the house and where at before we head in," I asked while everyone else was gearing up.

"Yea I have a new sonar program that I just finished that's not on the market. Now is the perfect time to test it out," he said.

"I just might have to put you on my payroll and get you away from cheap as Hector," I told him and he agreed.

It took him no time to launch the device and in a matter of 2 minutes we had a layout of the entire building. "Well the good thing is Brooklyn and Nessa are alive. The bad thing is the house is surrounded and with a lot of people," he said.

"How many people are we looking at," I finally asked him.

"At least 50 people," he said. When he said that I went right over to Hector and hit him dead in his mouth.

"Nigga it's over 50 people guarding her. What the fuck do you have in your closet. You better start talking now before you not live to see you first grandchild be born," I snapped with the gun in his face.

"Alright man chill. Get that shit out my face and give me a towel and I will tell you everything. You might want to sit down for this one too," he said.

"I'm not sitting for shit so start talking before you start floating," I said through clenched teeth.

"Well long story short the lady who raised Brooklyn was not her mom. Bella is her real mom. She had to skip town because of them and now she's back. The lady who was watching her was Bella sister Natasha. Natasha ended up getting strung out because she didn't know what to do with all the money she was receiving from us to watch Brooklyn and the kids. Egypt is also my child with Bella as well. Carter is Oscar child from Natasha and Elijah is Poppy's child from Natasha as well. The reason we came back early was because Natasha had got into some debt with Oscar. He tried to rap Brooklyn but that's when she killed him.

Oscar was Javier brother. Javier was only around because he brought the most money in and moved the most work. Had I known at the time that Brooklyn had killed Oscar then I would have killed Javier myself before this shit got out of hand. He's also after Brooklyn because they think she knows where my secret stash is if something was to ever happen to me," Hector told everyone.

"I feel like you leaving some shit out," I barked at him.

"Oh I am. Jigsaw is my son," he said and that's when Bella lost it.

"So we've been married for 20 years and you failed to mention that you had a son," she yelled while counting on her fingers. "

And you cheated too you dirty bastard," she yelled while smacking him in the face.

We all let them fight because nobody wanted to step in between that shit. I've heard my stories on Bella and she's not to be fucked with. She once killed a man because he short her 25 cent. "Are you two done fighting because most of everyone is leaving and it looks to only be 10 people guarding the girls now," Brian said. Everyone looked up and noticed that Javier must have had a meeting and sent everyone out to fine us.

"So where are they now?" I asked while still looking at the tracker on my phone.

"The girls are in a basement. There is two people on the couch in the living room and one person on the bedroom laying down. You hvae two peolpe out front and two poeple out back. There also looks to be three more people in the house on the third floor. Probably counting money," he said.

"Okay here's what we are going to do. "Hector you follow me we will go in through the basement window. Bella you stay here and if you see anyone run out the house dead them. I also need you to take out the two people out front. I've heard about your sniper skills. Jigsaw, you and Marcus take the backdoor. Knock thouse two people out and grab Javier out of the bedroom. Brian you and your team goes in through the front door and also the two people on the couch. Also I need at least 5 people out here to watch Bella's back as well," I told them.

"Is everybody in position?" I asked on the headset once we were all connected to. Once everyone said yes we rushed the house all at the same-time. When me and Hector went into the basement we found Brooklyn and Nessa in the corner curled up with each other sleeping. Brooklyn and Nessa had both been beaten pretty badly.

"Baby wake up. It's me and your dad we're here to take you and Nessa home," I told her shaking them out of their sleep. They went into defense mode so that let me know every time they came down here they were hitting on them.

"Who did this to you?" I asked her while cutting the ropes from around her legs, hands, and throat. All she could do was nod her head and cry into my arms.

"Nessa who did this to y'all," I asked since Brooklyn couldn't even talk. She looked up at me and started to cry.

"Come on Nessa you have to tell me something," I begged her.

"It was Sade and Zack. Please don't kill them they were forced to do it. They didn't even want to do it. Javier and Poppy made them do it.

I quickly looked up at Hector then back to Nessa. "Are you sure Poppy had a role to play in this," I asked again just to be safe.

"Yes, they're both playing you. They said that if they didn't get the money you stole from them they were going to kill us all. We heard them the entire time they were in the meeting. They are on their way to your house to find y'all. Lucas call your mom and tell her to leave now. They've already killed my people so you don't gave to warn them," she revealed and starting to cry just as Marcus came down the steps.

"We have Zack and Sade tied up Javier is dead," he told me in my ear.

"Well he's not the only problem Poppy is in on it too," I told him.

"Are you sure," he asked me sounding confused and surprised as I did.

"Yea man. Nessa said they ordered Sade and Zack to beat them and if Hector didn't give them the money he stole they were going to kill them," I told him.

Once we got the girls upstairs I put them in the back of my

truck and told them to sit tight. "Aye I called my mom but she's not answering," I told everyone as we put Javier in the field and burned his body.

"Nessa said they were headed to our house then my mom's house," I told them.

"Let's go. Keep the girls with us I don't trust anyone right now," Marcus said.

"You read my mind cause neither do I," I told him.

Marcus jumped in the truck with me as we raced to my mother's house. When we got there she was outside doing yard work. We had everyone else park a street over and come through the back yard into the house. Once everyone was inside my mom started yelling at us. "Lucas what the fuck is going and. AND WHY THE FUCK HAS BROOKLYN AND NESSA BEEN BEAT," she yelled at me.

"Ma chill Javier, Poppy, Zack, and Sade did this I told her.

"Where are they," she asked.

"Sade and Nessa are in the basement with the team now but don't go down there from what we were told Poppy and Javier forced them to do it. They didn't even want to do it. Poppy is on his way here Javier is already dead," I told her.

"Take the girls and go to the panic room now. Don't come out until me or Marcus come and get you," I told her.

Once they were in the panic room we had everyone in place waiting for Poppy and his crew to show up. Me and Marcus were in the attic window and we had a view of the entire street. We lived on a dead end and away from all of the other houses so we kind of hand an advantage plus the houses were so far apart you wouldn't know what was going on unless you were just being nosey. "You think Hector told us about everything," Marcus asked me.

"Man hell naw," I said while still looking out of the window.

"You see that," I asked Marcus while following the shadow.

"WE GOT ACTION," I said into the headset so that everyone could hear.

"I see 3 trucks in the back of the house," Hector said.

"I have two in the front Jigsaw said. "It should be a total of 6 one is missing," Brian said.

I was glad we had Brian on our team cause with the shit he had we could spot anyone from anywhere with this type of shit he had. "Snipe if you can I see 3 in the backyard in the field," Brian said.

"I got them," Bella said and just like that they were all out with head shots. She played no games and earned the nick name Beasty Bella back in the day. One by one she was hitting everyone in the field with a head shot. Poppy hadn't been around much and when he was Bella was never around so he didn't know she was back.

"The last car is approaching us," Brian said.

"Let Poppy come to us cause I have some questions to ask him," Hector said.

"They left they must know their team is dead," Brian said.

"Let's roll out to the warehouse," I told everyone. I went to the panic room and got my mom and the girls out. I was beating myself up on the inside with the way Brooklyn faced looked right now. Her left eye was swollen shut, her lip was busted, she had a hand print on her left cheek, and a food print on her back. I was thankful they didn't kick her in the stomach because I would have lost it if I lost my baby girl.

CHAPTER 9: I'M NOT TO BE PLAYED WITH

Brooklyn

When Javier and Zack snatched Nessa and I from my father's house I cursed myself because I knew Lucas was going to be mad at me. I cursed myself even more for leaving the house without my gun. When they threw us in the back of a truck I prayed the entire way. If I lost my baby girl I would never be the same. The drive to the place that took us felt like hours because I didn't want to pull my phone out and they say that I had it.

They drug us out the back of the truck into the basement

of a broken down home. Once inside they tied our hands and feet, and even put rope around our necks. If Lucas didn't find us alive I was going to hunt his ass for the rest of my life. When Lucas married me, I truly wondered did he know he married a crazy lady sometimes.

Once they had us tied up we saw Sade come down the steps and I immediately saw red. A part of me wonder if she knew they were going to do this or if she was just pulled into it by force either way she was getting fucked up once Lucas and Marcus found us. Poppy and Javier told them to beat us until we could no longer move. I could tell by the way they walked over to us they didn't want to do it. They stood there for a few minutes not wanting to touch us until Poppy and Javier said they didn't hear any screaming.

When Zack told me to cover my stomach I knew then he didn't want to hurt the baby. I also knew then that he was forced to do this, the both of them were. The blow he delivered to my face sent me over the roof. I cursed him from a to z and begged him to stop but they just kept going. It wasn't until Sade whispered to us and told us to fake pass out so they could stop and that's exactly what we did.

The pain we were in put us to sleep. I just hoped and prayed I woke up from the beating they put on us. When Lucas found us I went into defense mode because I thought they sent them down there to beat us again. I couldn't even talk when he was asking me who did this to us. Nessa had to tell him everything because I was beyond hurt. After he put us in the back of his truck we went to his moms house. The entire ride there I didn't say anything.

The moment his mom saw us she went off and I had never seen her snap like that before. They took us into the panic room because Poppy was the only one left they needed to get to and he was headed there looking for Lucas mom not knowing Lucas had already saved us. Now that they had killed everyone we were headed to the warehouse because they still didn't have Poppy and I am pretty sure Lucas didn't trust me staying put right now.

"Lucas I'm sorry," I told him from the back seat.

"Sorry for what?"

"For lying to you. I played sleep only because I wanted to surprise you with something since we had gotten married today," I told him truthfully.

"Baby never apologize for trying to do something for me. Next time make sure you tell me you left the house and you take your gun ok," he told me as he reached over and held onto my hand as he was driving.

"How's our baby girl doing," he asked while rubbing my belly.

"She's doing fine now. I think she slept through what was going on because now she is moving nonstop," I said.

"How's your face feeling?"

"It's okay. I don't really want to look at it to see how bad it looks," I confessed.

The look he gave me when I said that caused me to laugh. "You said that same shit when you was in the hospital and Ricky walked into the room," he said.

"How you know and you wasn't there," I asked confused.

"Baby you know he told me chill. You're beautiful regardless of how you look," he told me. The smile I had on my face could be seen for miles but once I felt the swelling I stopped and turned towards the window.

I watched as we passed by the trees and finally hit the warehouse. We had to let the team swipe the area first before we went in. "It's clear baby come on," Lucas said as he helped me out of the car because my back was hurting bad.

"Can you pick me up my back hurts," I said in my baby tone while doing my puppy dog face.

"You know I got wifey forever," he said as he kissed me on the lips then picked me up.

As he carried me up the steps I couldn't help but to take him in and admire him. "Let's go to the office and have a quick session," I whispered in his ear while licking it at the same time. The way his eyes got big tickled the hell out of me.

"Sorry baby I can't do that because you're already in pain," he told me and of course I got mad. I rolled my eyes and smacked my lips and of course the nigga thought the shit was funny. He sat me at the table and went and got me something to eat from out the fridge. At times they had works her 24/7 so they kept the fridge her socked. Even on nights when he had big shipments he would nap in his office on the bed in there then get right back to work because he had a lot of work to do.

I slowly made my way up to his office because I needed to lay down. When I got in there he was on the phone with someone but I couldn't tell who because his back was turned. He didn't even hear me walk in. "I can't right now I'm with my wife. I told you I would come back through later on tonight," he said. I walked closer so I could hear who he was talking to and my heart broke once I realized it was another female.

I FELL IN LOVE WITH THE PLUG 3

"Look bitch you knew what it was from the jump. I don't love you I love my wife now learn your role and stay in it," he said into the phone. I pulled the gun from my waist and shot him in his shoulder and leg.

"You tell that bitch she can have you if you don't bleed out first," I cried then stormed away. I ran all the way to the car pushing everyone out my way who tried to stop me. They saw my gun so that was probably the only reason why I made it to the truck without being stopped.

My mind was so clouded I didn't even realized I was crying until I was outside in the car driving away. His mother started blowing my phone up but I wasn't going to answer it. I threw my phone out the window and headed towards town. The one thing I loved the most just did the worst thing he could ever do to me. I always thought shit with us was too good to be true. Now look at me hurt and shit because I ignored my gut feelings all along.

First, I went to the bank to empty all of his accounts. He had me so fucked up right now that I would rather be dead than alive. The second stop was the condo. The car that I got for him was going back but I needed to get a few things from the house beforehand. It was going on 2am and I knew he was probably going off that he couldn't find me right now. The tracking device he hand in my earrings I had threw out the window by a hotel just to throw him off track.

I checked into the Drury Plaza Hotel in Franklin and got a suite because I didn't know how long I would be staying here. "Can you also make sure no one knows that I am staying here," I told the lady at the front desk.

"Sure thing. If you want I can check you in as anonymous guest or VIP guest so they know not to give anyone any info on you," she said to me.

"That would be wonderful. I'm hiding from my husband," I told her in a low town and when I finally looked up I assumed she saw my face because she said she would flag my account to where only the manager on duty would bring anything to me that I called to ask for.

I rode the elevator to the top floor and finally retired to the room for the rest of the night. I turned every light in the room on. I took the chair and put it under the door to where no one could get in if they tried and also but the chain, along with the do not disturb sign up. When I walked into the bathroom I was in awe at the sight of it. The tub was about to put me to sleep and it didn't even know it. While my bath water ran I turned the news on to see if anything was going on and they only thing that caught my eye was a house fire because the house looked familiar but I couldn't tell who's it was because it was burnt to the ground.

The sound that was coming from the hall caused me to jump clean out my skin. I ran and turned all the lights off except for the bathroom light then looked through the peephole to see who it was. Luckily for me it was room service going to the room across the hall from me so I went into the bathroom to soak in the tub. The hot water felt so relaxing to my body that I didn't realize had fallen asleep until I got cold and started to shiver.

The time on the clock said 6:45am and the sand man was tugging at my eyes. Once I got out of the cold water I let it out the tub then turned the shower on so I could just shower and sleep. When I finished I brushed my teeth then walked out of the bathroom. The sun coming through the window almost blinded me so I pulled the shades back then climbed into the bed. Not even 5 minutes later I was asleep.

One would have thought on the outside looking in I was living the best and happiest life but truth be told I was living the worst life ever. My father had been lying to me about my mother this entire time and the woman who was actually raising me was not my mother. A lot of things started to make sense on why she treated me the worst. I understood everything now. My brain was a wreck with so many questions that I didn't even get to sleep like I wanted to. My attitude was on 10 and I needed to stay far away from Lucas before I ended up killing him.

• •

Lucas

Right now I felt like the dumbest person on Earth. Here I am sitting in the hospital trying to get stitched up while everyone is asking me a million questions. "What did you do to Brooklyn to make her shoot you?" Hector asked me for the 100th time.

"Man I don't fucking know," I barked at him. When he finally left the room I motioned for my mom to shut the door so no one else could come in. After she did that she pulled her chair next to my bed and I knew that look was her way of asking what happened and I better not lie.

I looked at my mom and just shook my head. "Ma I fucked up and I don't think we can bounce back from this," I told her.

"I'm no mind reader son so tell me what you did," she told me with a cold tone. To be honest I think she knew but she still wanted me to tell her anyway.

I took a deep breath and said, "She found out I was chea....." and before I could finish my statement she smacked the taste out of my mouth.

"Lucas Jenkins are you fucking crazy. That's your wife now

and she's pregnant how could you do her like that," she barked at me.

Right now I didn't even have the courage to look my mom in the eye but I had no choice unless I wanted to be smacked again. "You better be lucky the poor child didn't kill you. She's probably somewhere crying her eyes out right now waiting for you to make it better," she told me.

"Nah ma. She changed her number and emptied the bank accounts. I tracked her at a hotel downtown but she's not checked in there. I have my people looking in every ditch and hotel they can to find her and they have nothing," I confused but trying not to cry.

Yes I loved my wife but when shit got tuff, my guard was down and I was weak. I meet this hoe name Roxie in the strip club. She gave me a private dance and we ended up fucking and we haven't stopped since then. She knew about Brooklyn and she also knew to never call me that I would call her but word got around in the streets that me and Brooklyn got married and she called me crying saying it was suppose to be her.

Like any other nigga I fed her false hope just to fuck her because she fucked me good. I wasn't really digging her because she couldn't cook and she also didn't keep her house clean either. I found out she had a kid she didn't take care of and that was a major turn off but I thought with my dick and she was just a fuck. I held my hand in my hands trying to process and think of any place she might be right now. When I heard the door shut I looked up and noticed my mother left and didn't say anything to me.

My mother never left without telling me bye and I knew for a fact that she hated me right now cause she use to do my father the exact same way when he cheated on her. When Marcus came into the room I put him up on game and she just shook his head at me. "Man I have to find her go get the doctor so I can go," I told him.

"I think it's best you stay because she just might finish your ass off at this point," he said. I pulled the IV out my arm and pulled the rest of the stuff they had on me off. I grabbed my clothes got dressed.

Once I came out the bathroom the doctor and nurse had my discharge papers ready for me to go. I had Marcus take me back to the condo so I could figure out my next move.

"So what are you going to do about Brooklyn man," he asked finally breaking the silence in the car.

"Man I don't even know. I have no clue on where to find her because she didn't go to any hotel cause her name is not on the books. They've checked all of the old houses and condos and didn't find any trace of her," I told him while I pinched the bridge of my nose and fought back tears.

"Just let sis blow of her steam I'm sure she will come around soon."

"Shid that girl can stay mad for weeks. I wouldn't be surprised if she already had the divorce papers filed.

When Marcus laughed at that I wanted to smack him but it was my own fault that I was in the situation. "Bruh look here man. You know she loves you and will do anything for you. Like I said let her blow her steam. When she comes back yo ass better have some shit planned for her and you better not do that shit ever again," he preached to me. I just nodded my head cause it wasn't shit I could do right now until I found her.

"Aye who vet is that?" Marcus asked me. "

Mine. That's what she wanted to surprise me with but she ended up getting snatched by Javier," I told him.

"Damn man. Well I'm fina got put Nessa to sleep I'll be back in a few hours bruh," he told me as we slapped hands and I got on the elevator. Instead of going to the condo we shared together I went to mine to shower and get changed. When I got out the shower I heard someone knocking at the door. Long and behold it was Roxie and I was not about to answer it.

What seemed like 20 minutes later she finally stopped knocking and left. I waited for another 10 minutes before I left and took the stairwell to the condo I shared with Brooklyn. Once inside I could tell she had been there because her suitcase was gone. I started punching holes in the wall now that I was alone when I should've been beating the life out of Roixe because she knew damn well not to call me. Once I finally snapped out of it I realized I had messed the wall up and my knuckles were bleeding.

Sitting down at the table I started to clean my hands just as Marcus and Ricky walked through the door. They both looked at me and shook their head at me. "Man don't come in here judging me and shit," I told them.

"Man ain't nobody judging yo dumb as," Ricky said.

"But can I asked you one thing?" Marcus asked.

"Yeah man what's up," I said while wrapping my had up.
He looked at me with seriousness in his eyes and asked, "Was it worth man?" I knew what he meant by that and to be honest it wasn't.

"Fuck no. I got a pregnant wife sitting somewhere alone crying her eyes out right now because of the shit I did to her," I confessed.

Finally it was time to get back to work. Brooklyn was a grown woman and she knew where home was. As bad as I wanted to chase after her I had to get this shipment checked in first then I would go look for her. We headed to the warehouse to check everything in. Once I made sure we had our guns and drugs, including the right amount I jetted out the door to go find my wife. It had been 48 hours without her and I was starting to go crazy. "Remember what I told you Lucas," Marcus yelled as I got to the door. I through my hand up and walked out.

I've been calling my mom's phone the past 48 hours and she hasn't answered. I was sure she had found Brooklyn and that was the only reason why she had yet to answer her phone. Since I couldn't tracked Brooklyn I tracked my mom and it was showing her location at a hotel in Franklin. I'm not sure why she's there when they had already checked and was told she wasn't there already.

I pulled my blunts out the consul and headed towards my mom's location. Something in my mind told me to call her again and this time she finally answered. "Ma look before you go off just hear me out. I did that shit when I was at a low point in life. You have to believe me when I say I love Brooklyn. When the bitch called me I was going over there to actually kill her because she wouldn't leave me alone and I didn't want her to come in between what me and Brooklyn had. She's my wife and I'm going to love her until the day I take my last breath just please tell me she's ok. I know you're with her I tracked you phone to Franklin," I told her.

She didn't say anything when I stopped talking so I had to take the phone off my ear to make sure the call was still connected and it was. "Look I know she probably doesn't want to talk to me, but just tell her that I love her and I'm sorry." I didn't even give her time to respond before I ended the call. I did a U-turn and headed back to my condo. A part of me wish I never did what I did and a part of me was telling me to go get my wife, but I learned one thing from my father and that was to never go near a woman when they almost tried to kill you until you were sure they had calmed down.

For all I care she could have had my mom try to shoot me but I know she wouldn't turn on me. When I got home I started fixing the wall that I had messed up and ordered some pizza hoping that she would come home. My mom never called back and her phone was still pinging at the hotel in Franklin. The 48 hours quickly turned into two weeks and I slept, ate, and breath nothing but work and home. We had yet to find Poppy and it was as if he was hiding right now.

Marcus and Ricky came by every day to check on me because I really wasn't leaving the house anymore. My mom stopped by but only to get some things for Brooklyn. She still wasn't talking to me and I didn't blame her. I pulled some fuck boy shit and I was even mad at myself. But they always say if you do bullshit be ready to deal with the actions brought with it.

Today was Sunday and I knew my mom was coming over to get Brooklyn some more clothes. She came once a week to get her things and it was always on Sunday's. When she let herself in she came into the living room where I was and sat right next to me on the couch. "Son you know I love you and Brooklyn. I would do anything to see you two back together but you tore that girl heart into pieces. I don't know how you plan on fixing it but you need to start doing something and I mean now. She wants to come home but she's afraid that she's going to shoot you again. I listen to that girl cry herself to sleep every single night because of you. I will say this she loves you but it's like both of y'all are waiting to see who's going to be the bigger person and it needs to be you. Last night she cried because she wants to come home and you have yet to come and get her," she told me. I looked up and her and I could tell that she was tired.

"Ma why didn't you tell me earlier?"

"Because she made me promise not to tell you. But after today she needs to be home. She's hardly eating and she's stressing and it's not good for the baby."

"Where is she I will go get her now?"

"She's at the Drury Plaza Hotel in the penthouse room 7658," said while giving me the key card to her room.

"Don't call my phone until y'all make up. I'm going to cook y'all dinner then go home my old as is tired," she told me as she pushed me off the couch to get dressed.

I jetted into my bathroom to take a shower so I didn't go over there all funky. Once I finished I brushed my teeth and flossed as well. I grabbed my clippers and gave myself an edge up as well. After I checked my appearance in the mirror I jetted to the closet to get dressed. I put on my Tom Ford fitted suit because I knew she loved me in this and she picked it out for me as well. A few minutes later I grabbed my Tom Ford cologne, sprayed it on, then headed to the Ranger Rover.

On the way there I stopped and got her a dozen of pink, white, and purple roses. When I got back to the car I made sure I had the keycard then headed to the hotel. I was a nervous wreck to go pick up my own damn wife and I had to shake my head at that. My phone started ringing which snapped me out of my thoughts and I quickly answered it. "Hello"

"Aye hurry up man mama said she cooked and I'm trying to come over since Asia don't cook," Ricky yelled into.

"Nigga I'm pulling up at the hotel now take yo ass on over

there and eat shit," I barked into the phone and hung it up.

I valet the car then grabbed the roses and headed towards Brooklyn room. Even though I had the keycard I still knocked on the door but she didn't answer. I used the key to let myself in the went into the bedroom and found her asleep. She looked so peaceful that I didn't even want to wake her up. I sat the flowers down in the living room then went back into the bedroom. I undressed then climbed into the bed with her. The scent of her body almost brought me to tears because I missed it so much.

I grabbed her into my arms and she still didn't move. I put my hand on her belly and felt the baby going wild in there. It seems like it woke her up but she still didn't move. The energy in the room was there but also the sadness. When I put my hand on her thigh she moved it back to her belly. She started to talk but when I heard her crying I sat up and pulled her into my arms. At that point she was balling and couldn't even get her words out.

The way she cried ate at me to know that I was the one causing her this pain. I'm supposed to hurt anyone that hurts her yet the one causing her the pain right now is me. I picked her up bridal style and carried her into the shower. I didn't care that my suit was getting wet I only cared right now to fix what I had wronged. She was crying so bad that she was burning up and turning red in the face. She clung to me as if she thought I was going to die if I left out the door without her.

"Brooklyn!!!" I barked at her trying to get her to snap out of the daze she was in. She had been crying nonstop to the point to where she was hyperventaling. The look in her eyes screamed I hate you and I love you. They also screamed to kill you or not to kill you. The energy in the room screamed for me to leave but I was not going to go.

Her bone straight hair was now curly and sticking to her

face. I peeled the layer of clothes off of her while eye fucking her. Once she was completely naked I placed her on the bench in the shower the peeled out of my Tom Ford suit layer by layer. I pulled her up to join me under the shower head because at this point no words needed to be said. The scent of the hotel soap burned my nose until I found her body wash on the bathroom sink.

She looked up at me then her soap and I knew I had to get my ass out the shower and not question her about it. I washed us both up twice then turned the shower off. The plush towel felt so good against my skin that I didn't want to put clothes on. I really didn't have a choice since my suit was wet and needed to dry. It seemed like it took me 5 minutes to find the lotion in Brooklyn suitcase so that I could lotion us up. After I lotioned myself up I took her towel off of her as she laid down naked on the bed. My mind went into overdrive as I started to stare at her ass. The baby oil gel was about to do her body good once I finished with her.

My hands roamed her body because they had really missed her. Mentally I was fucking the shit out of her physically I was just rubbing her down. The stress she was under could be felt leaving her body because she was no longer tense. The massage I was giving her ass had her pussy leaking with juices. One thing about my baby she got wet easily for me. The way her pussy was smiling at me I couldn't help but find my way to her.

As soon as my lips touched her she let out a small moan. See the only thing I ever wanted to do was to please her. I never wanted to cause my baby any pain but like a nigga I thought with my dick at a point when I was at my lowest and it should have never even gotten that far. Hell truth be told the bitch should have never even gotten my damn number. "UMMMMMMM!!!!!" Brooklyn said as I licked her like a kitten licking milk from a bowl.

Her juices we running down my beard and I didn't even bother to wipe it away. I inserted my index and middle finger into her vagina and slow fucked her while sucking on her pearl. The way she was grinding on my tongue was turning me on. "Baby I'm so sorry," I said in between slurps sending her body to its peak. Baby girl was dripping like a faucet. My head bobbed up and down as she guided me with her hands.

When I tried to come up for air she wouldn't let me. I let her take control. I picked her up as she held onto my head and ate away as she sat on my shoulders. The second I sat on the bed I laid down and let her mount my face. She found her pace on my tongue and rode it to her climax. The way she shivered let me know I was doing it right because she came so hard she was crying. I locked my arms around her thighs to keep her from getting up and kept licking her away. I was sucking the stress out of her soul because she needed it. "Why did you have to hurt me," she asked in between sobs.

The vibration from my response made her come again but this time she was squirting. When our eyes connected as I licked away ever drop the connection between us was still there but also the sadness. "Brooklyn" I called out to her as she turned her back to me.

"What Lucas"

"Bring your as here I am not done with you," I told her. She came and sat her naked body on my lap and played with the one thing that missed her the most, my dick.

I lifted her by the chin and looked her dead in the eyes and told her, "I'm sorry that I hurt you. I didn't fuck that girl raw and I also didn't eat that girl out. This tongue is for you and only you. To be safe I even flushed the condom down the toilet. You don't deserve any of the pain I caused you and if you want a divorce and want to leave then I will let you. I should be putting a smile on your face not tears because I couldn't keep my dick in my pants.

So what do you want to do?"

She mounted me the smacked me. The way she bounced up and down on my dick had me ready to come already. "I want you Lucas, but I will not share you. You're dick belongs to me and no one else. Look at me when I'm talking to you Lucas," she demanded me.

"Man if I look at you I will explode," I told her truthfully. When she stopped riding me I finally opened my eyes. They had been sitting in the back of my head because I was not ready to nut yet. Her tongue invaded my mouth and mine did the same to hers. I held her face with both my hands as she rode me to my climax and I moaned like a bitch.

My heavy breathing was found funny to her and I hated that shit. When she got up I smacked her ass. She grabbed my hand and lead me to the shower. "Why did she call your phone Lucas? Don't give me no bullshit ass answer either!"

I took a deep breath and said, "She found out you and I got married. I didn't give her any false hope. She caught feelings for the dick. I even told her if I found you alive she was cut off. The crazy part is that I only fucked her once," I told her truthfully while looking her in the eyes.

"I believe you," she told me.

"Did you not once think it's funny how she called you the day I went missing," she asked me. I rubbed my chin because she was on to something.

"Hurry up and shower we're about to go pay Roxie a visit," I told her. The sinister smile she plastered on her face lets me know Roxie will no longer be alive after this visit and I was fine with that.

Luckily Wanda had just got back in town so I told her to be on standby and ready when he headed towards Roxie's crib. "Lucas I love you but when you think with yo dick you do dumb shit," she told me. I mugged her and told her to shut up before the conversation quickly went left. She folded her arms and yelled ugh like I was supposed to get mad.

It took me a minute to remember how to get to her house and when I did Brooklyn went crazy. "I clearly married the dumbest bitch on earth," she barked while hitting me nonstop even though the punches didn't hurt.

"CHIL WITH THAT BITCH WORD." I yelled as I snatched her as up by her shirt. It didn't faze her because she socked me in my eye then threw her wedding ring at me. I slammed on the breaks and almost knocked her head off her shoulders.

"Brooklyn I will let that stupid shit you just did slide this time because I know you are still made at me, but one thing you are to never dude it take that fucking wedding ring of period. Throw that again and yo ass will be Brooklyn Taylor Johnson before the ink dries," I said as I got in her space with my finger pushing her forehead back.

Her attitude made me love her and hate her at the same time. I felt like she pushed certain buttons at times to see how far she could go. I could tell I scared her because she didn't move until I was back on my side of the car and driving again.
"You know I'm not scared of you dude," Brooklyn said.

I gave her the side eye and told her to shut the fuck up cause her mouth was starting to piss me off. "I don't expect you to be Brooklyn."

Between her attitude, her mouth, and her mood swings I didn't know how to come towards her these days. "That's her house over there," When Brooklyn looked up she gave me the dirtiest look ever.

"Take me to Hector's house he has some explaining to do," she said. I did an illegal U-turn and head towards his home not asking any questions.

The moment we pulled into the driveway she was jumping her ass out the car and jetting to the front door. I already knew this shit was about to get worse before it got better. Before she hit the door god enough I snatcher her back by her shirt. "Hop out the truck like that again while you're carrying our daughter and watch what I do to your little ass," I threatened her through clenched teeth.

"How about you threaten this pussy when we leave since you keep turning me on," she told me. I had to fix my pants because that girl always knew what she was doing.

"Don't be in their dry snitching either," I yelled after her when she walked off.

CHAPTER 10: FAMILY PROBLEMS

Hector

The way Brooklyn treated that boy he was going to get sick of her shit and leave one day. I watched the altercation on the screen before she came running in the house. When Lucas snatched her ass up I started laughing because he was finally putting his damn foot down. If I didn't put him up on game she was going to be his bitch and run him way and to be honest I was tired of her cleaning my accounts every damn day. I loved my daughter very much but she had a shopping problem and needed rehab for is asap.

"DADDY!!!," Brooklyn yelled while running through the front door.

"Stop all that damn yelling I'm in the office," I pretty much yelled back at her. When she walked into the office Lucas was right behind her mugging her like always.

"Had I not known y'all one would think y'all are brother and sister the way you to fight," I teased him as he took a seat.

"Do you remember Roxie?' Brooklyn asked me. I watched Lucas face expression out the corner of my eye and knew what was up and I had to save him.

"Umm, if you're speaking of the girl you're uncle use to talk to then yes I do. Why what about her?" I asked while pouring Lucas and I both a shot of hen.

"Your son in law fucked her but that's beside the fact. Did you know she's been snooping around looking for me. Funny how she finds Lucas every time I pop up missing. Do you think Javier has her stalking us?" she asked. I cut my eye towards Lucas and he shrugged his shoulders.

"It wouldn't surprise me. She is usually looking for her next come up," I added as I pointed towards Lucas.

"Wow the tempers in this room need some help," Bella said when she walked in. Lip smacking was all that could be heard from Brooklyn before the room erupted into laughter.

"I swear yawl make me sick," she said while stuffing her face with food.

"Now that you two are here I need to make a confession," I stated while lighting a blunt.

"Brooklyn do you remember the night we had the cookout

and I sent you off with Lucas?" I asked even though she wasn't paying me any attention. She was too busy twirling in her hair and eye fucking Lucas as if me and her mother were not even in the room.

"July 4, yeah I remember," she said not even looking at me. I cleared my throat and she finally looked at me cause I was not about to tell this story twice.

"Damn daddy I said I heard you go on with the fucking story," she barked at me.

"First off, watch who the fuck you talking to. I'm not Lucas I'll beat your ass! Now as I was saying. I confronted Javier about stealing from me and told him after Jamaica that we would no longer be business partners. He thought that you would know where I kept my stash but you didn't. Well you do but you just wouldn't have access to it until next year. The only person who knew about my stash was Lucas. The money is hidden in a safe incase something happens to me you and Jigsaw will want for nothing and I mean nothing at all. I didn't know about Jigsaw or Egypt until I came back and laid eyes on the both of them. For a while we thought you were our only child but yea I got around back in the day so that might even be more siblings of yours around here," I told her.
I am pretty sure Bella wants to smack the fuck out of me right now but her ass will live for the time being. I did have a set of twins but their mom didn't want this lifestyle so I have no clue or what state she's in right now.

"So all of this is because Lucas took his spot, you cut him off, and he's just money hungry. Well Hector you're not a god liar so spill the rest of it," Brooklyn said.

"Alright fine you win. Don't start all that bullshit ass crying either,"

"I'm not you're real father Javier is. You would have thought her eyes were going to pop out her head the way she spit her juice out and dropped her plate.

"Yawl lie so fucking much I don't even know what to believe," she said.

"Brooklyn, he's telling the truth," Bella told her.

She sprinted out of the room and I was not going to chase after her. Lucas could but I don't. "No Lucas, let her mother run after her. You and I need to talk." I waited until Bella left to finish the conversation.

"After this last deal I'm going legit how about you?"

"Yeah man I'm done. I'm just ready to move far away from all of this shit. I'm tired of shit happening to her and I am also tired of seeing her in pain. I can't keep painting the city red because if I do the feds will pop up just like they did when Bella had to lay low. I got Brooklyn for life along with our child too I just need to keep them safe at all times. I know my girl can hold her own but she does not need all of that blood on her hands. That's what she has me for.," he told me.

"Man look I have an exit plan that only includes Brooklyn, Bella, Jigsaw, you, and myself. We will go over plans soon once I get this crybaby out her feelings," I stated just as Brooklyn came back into the room with them fake ass tears.

With the bullshit Brooklyn always pulled on me as a kid she should be on someone's TV show. Maybe if she earns some Grammy's with the stupid reactions she be having to shit I could leave the game forever. Who am I kidding I love this fast-easy money I thought to myself. After these plans of mines take action my family will be set for life.

****

Brooklyn

My so called not father Hector tried to keep me blind to a lot of shit but I was far from blind in fact I saw all the shit that was going on. In my eyes Hector was and will always be my father. He raised me and was always there for me no matter what. For instance, I knew Natasha was not my mom. Reason being the way she treated me and the energy was always off. Hector always came running when she treated me wrong up until he faked his death then Lucas or Javier would do for me but mainly Lucas.

Right now, I was blown at that fact that Javier was my father and I actually thought that was a lie. The only reason why I ran out of the room crying was because of the way he use to treat me if he knew I was his child. To also know that my uncle, my own flesh and blood sexually assaulted me years back and tried to rape me really put me into my feelings. They do say family is your worst enemy and this shit is true.

With my head cocked to the side I didn't know if I wanted to smack Lucas or knock his head clean the fuck off right now. This is the reason why I think I'm crazy or have a few issues. One minute my mind is in one place then the next minute it's somewhere else. Everyone says it's the baby but I really haven't been right since Hector Jr. beat my ass. I might just be over reacting but whatever. "Lucas I'm…. "Either hungry or sleepy huh," he answered before I could finish. I hated when he would cut me of and finish what I saying.

I really wanted to go out to eat but when he came back in the room with pizza I figured that would do for now. I was so busy stuffing my face I didn't even see Nessa come into the room and sit right next to me.

"I called your phone earlier, thought you were sleep until Marcus said you were over here and drug me out the house with him," she told me.

"Damn my bad. My phone is in the kitchen. I guess you been in the house since they saved us too huh?" I asked while pushing the pizza box her way.

"Girl yes. Marcus only got me out the house today cause you were here. If you weren't I would be at home in the bed."

"Hell me too Nessa. Let's go in the living room while they talk about shit."

When we got in the living room we plopped down on the couch with my pink blanket and turned the TV on. "So, I caught Lucas cheating," I finally confessed to Nessa.

"Bitch are you serious?" she asked me while spitting out her drink because I caught her of guard with it.

"Okay the real question is with you?"

"Bitch with Roxie, Javier old hoe. For some odd reason I think she has something to do with what's been going on. Like you only call Lucas when I'm missing so it just makes me wonder," I told her.

"Come on we're going for a ride," she said while dragging me of the couch.

"Where are we going?"

"To pay Roxie a visit."

The evil grin the appeared across my face would have scared anyone staring at me but Nessa was use to it now. "What if they come out looking for us?"

"Bitch you getting scary on me now. You're usually the one that's ready to wild out. Just tell them we're going to get some food duh," she said while playfully hitting my arm. I texted Lucas but he didn't text back so we left anyway.

On the ride over to the club my head was spinning. Nessa's uncle owned the place so we could be in and out and not be touched by anyone in there. I spotted her car as soon as we pulled up and a bitch quickly went to work. I slashed 3 of her tires and busted all the windows out. I even put oil and sugar in her gas tank and keyed the fuck out of her car. After today this bitch was going to know that Lucas Lee Jenkins was off limits and mine forever. We both walked in and sat at the bar until we spotted our victim.

"These niggas will fuck anything I swear," I told Nessa.

"Right. I mean she does have a nice ass but that's it," she said while literally staring at the girls ass.

"I mean yea she does. But it's still fuck that bitch cause she fucked my husband," I said in a low tone. When we peeped she was gong to her car we ordered a drink and sat at the bar like normal people. The second she came running back in crying, screaming, "Someone trashed my car Spiky!"

"And what the fuck that got to do with me Roxie?" he harshly said to her. She stomped her feet and headed to the locker room so I downed my water and headed towards the locker room too.

I put the clip into my gun, cocked it back, then went into the dressing room looking for my victim. She was in the corner on the phone crying her eyes out. "Lucas if I found out your bitch did this to my car so help me god her and your ugly as baby will pay," she said in a angry tone. I heard him yell back into the phone threating her and she looked as if she saw a ghost and hung it up.

"His bitch A.K.A. his wife is right here behind you," I said in a calm tone while screwing the silencer on.

Nessa locked the dressing room door so that it was just the three of us in there.

"You see if I wasn't pregnant I would beat the fuck out of you. But since I am I'm going to fill you with lead until you learn your place which is with my uncle Javier not my husband Lucas." Her heavy breathing was showing me how scared she truly was. *SPAT!!!! SPAT!!!!* Was the sound of my nine going off and me releasing a single bullet two both of her knee caps.

"Please don't shot me anymore I'll stay away I promise," she begged while trying to crawl away from me.

"Oh you will. I just need some information from you though. Get your ass up we're going for a ride," I told her while snatching her off the ground.

We went out the back door straight to the car. Roxi was on child safety lock so her as wasn't going to go anywhere. When we pulled back up to my fathers house they were still going over plans to go legit. "I HAVE A GUEST," I yelled before I dragged Roxi into the house. When Lucas looked at me I shrugged my shoulders at him. Lucas help me," she begged him.

"Bitch don't play with me," he told her. He squatted down

and snatcher her up by her hair and spat, "Who keeps coming after Brooklyn?"

"Fuck you. I aint telling you shit," she said.

"Take her to the basement," Hector told Lucas.

"He aint touching that bitch but you can take her down there," I told my dad while sizing him up.

My dad rolled his eyes an dragged Roxi like a rag doll all the way downstairs to the sound proof room. Hector clearly forgot that I was the one running shit around here. I like being pregnant because everything was clearly going my way. I was giving out orders as if I was the one calling shots when I know I really wasn't. I think they only gave me my way because they were tired of be crying and acting like a spoiled ass brat. Once I dropped I knew this special treatment was going to end so I was going to use it to my advantage for now.

Bella and Nessa tied Roxi to the chair while I grabbed one and sat right across from her. I smacked her cause she was going in and out of consciousness. Lucas looked as if he wanted to say something so I checked him quickly, "You got a problem Lucas? I'll sit your ass in a chair next to her and do you the same way, so get that dumb ass look off your face before I smack it off," I barked at him.

"Girl shut yo ass up. That shit turning me on. Hurry up so we can go home and I can tear your ass up." My face turned red because I was embarrassed that he said that in front of my parents.

"Girl we're all grown how you think you got here. Now hurry up cause I have to give ya father some act right," my mom said and I officially got grossed out.

I quickly put my attention back on Roxi and she was looking at us as if we were crazy.

"This is like a sport to us if you were wondering," I told her. The look on her face let me know that she was in fact scared and I had here right where I wanted her now.

"So are you going to tell me what I want to know or what?"

"Under one condition."

"Does it look like we are going to give you anything right now," I told her.

"Look I just want to make sure my son is not hurt in the process. Just at least help me relocate after I tell you everything," she begged.

"Okay," and just like that she believed me. She was going to relocated alight, to the bottom of the damn Cumberland River.

To make it even more real I threw a duffle bag full of cash at her feet with all 100's in them. Her eyes lit up like a kid on Christmas and I knew she was falling for my bait yet again.

"Okay so I meet Javier one night striping. He took me back to his house and we've been fucking around since then. He told me how he was going to take over your operation and leave you all for dead," said while looking at all of us.

"We already knew. Tell us something we don't know before I put a hot one in your head."

"He was using Terria and Serria as bait to get close to y'all to see where Hector secret stash was at.

With pity in my eyes I saw, "Awe poor lil tink tink. They set you up for the kill. There is no stash. Terria and Serria were handled a long time ago. So say goodbye," I said while holding the gun to her head and smiling.

"Okay okay wait. Poppy plans to raid this place Friday at 3am. He said he knows the stash is here somewhere and he will find it."

"Is that all," I said while coking the gun back.

"Yes one more thing. Did Lucas tell you he was the father of my son."

All I saw was red when I pulled the trigger. Roxi had just had a baby 8 months ago around the time I had gotten pregnant. I spun around and shot him in his chest. "BROOKLYN WHAT THE FUCK MAN," he yelled back at me but it fell on deaths ears. It seems like the so called man I thought I had and was in love with was a full hoe out here in these streets.

"LEAVE," I yelled at everyone in the room. You would think Lucas was tired of being shot by me but clearly he wasn't.

Once everyone walked out the room I walked over towards him and put my index finger in the hole in his chest and dug into it. "AUGH MAN GET THE FUCK ON WITH THAT STUPID SHIT," he yelled back while trying to get me off top of him.

"I'll see you in hell," I said calmly before I shot him again then turned the gun on myself. I wasn't into to sharing my man so if he was going to die then so was I.

CHAPTER 11: DEATH IS NEVER THE ANSWER
Bella

The moment we heard the gun go off again we all rushed back into the room with a team of doctors we had on call. The second she shot Lucas I sent the alert out for them to get there ASAP and they walked in as soon and Brooklyn shot herself. Her emotions were everywhere and I saw this coming the second she killed Roxi. Hector was going crazy and their was nothing I could do to calm him down. The doctors put us out the room so that they could work because we were just in the way.

When they came from out of the room they all looked defeated. "I'm so sorry Bella but there is nothing more that we can do. They're both dead," he said with a sincere voice. The only thing that could be heard was the cries from Nessa and myself. Hector left the house. He was to distraught to stand around and watch them carry them out in body bags. As a girl she had always told Lucas that if she couldn't have him to herself then no one could.

I hated that she thought I was never around but truth be told I was closer than she thought. At the time I had to lay low I changed my name and did plastic surgery to look like a new person that she had come to know as Catia her auntie. I always wanted to tell her who I was but that would put me at risk for going to jail for life and risk the cartel finding me. I had knocked off the grandson of the head operator of the Gonzales Cartel and they wanted my entire family to pay. They didn't know I was married to their other son Hector because they knew nothing of him. The only one who knew was his mother Sandra which was Juan mother as well. I killed Juan because he had raped me when we were suppose to be making a run.

The day of the run I was actually suppose to tell him about Hector but he had other plans instead. When I had awaken from what he done I was the in the hospital. Sandra was the one that found us because she knew the type of person he was. She had only helped me because she knew I was Hectors wife. She promised me that if I survived she would help me anyway she could and she did. She was the real connect and we also didn't even have to pay for the shit.

When the time was right she would explain everything to her husband and father but wanted to wait until the tension had died down. I got a phone call from her two days ago and was suppose to head to Mexico with Brooklyn, Lucas, and Hector so they could meet everyone but now they're dead and it's only going to be me and Hector.

I cursed myself for not telling him about it earlier because maybe all of this could have been prevented. After they carried them off I took Nessa home then headed to Lucas mother house. When I walked in the sadness in her face was enough to feel the entire room up. Everyone had arrived at her home so that we could make preparations for the funeral for them. "They always said one could never live without the other now look at them," sobbed Hector when he walked into the room.

He was never the type to shed a tear but with Brooklyn killing herself he was hurting bad right now. His slurred speech let me know that he had relapsed and starting drinking again. When Brooklyn was a girl he had gotten so drunk one night he beat her till she almost stopped breathing and he had vowed to never drink again. The moment he fell into my arms his flood gates had opened.

The tears he released were of a hurting father. Although we never tested Brooklyn to see who she belonged to he felt the need to take cause of her because Javier was unfit and also a rapist who raped his on kids. You never heard of his kids because they all killed themselves at young ages because of the things he did to them. His son Javier Jr took it the worst. He raped him then forced him to rape his sisters and had also gotten them pregnant. The day they all committed suicide they tried to kill Hector to but he was pulled from the fire in time by a firefighter just in time.
When he was in the hospital he would say he still saw his kids which lets us know they were gone they were haunting his ass. Had he tried that shit on Brooklyn, Hector would never had forgive himself for reveling the truth about it. That was a door that was suppose to stay sealed for life some now it was opened.

I was lost in a daze until Hector passed out drunk on Mrs. Jenkins floor. "Jigsaw can you help me put your father in the car?"

"Yes ma'am," he replied. For him to be Hector's child he was the sweetest one I had ever meet. Hector Jr was an animal and well Brooklyn had a mouth of a sailor but I loved my baby girl.

"If you want I can help you with him tonight. I have nothing to do other then pick up my baby sisters from my aunts house," he told me.

"That would be prefect because I'm going to catch hell getting him in the shower. You can ride with us," I told him.

We had to go over to the projects to pick them up and I immediately got mad at the condition that they were living in. I understand he just found out this was his son but he should not be living like this with his sisters period. When he brought them to the car they were all asleep so when they woke up in the morning I just knew what to do. "Jigsaw if you don't mind me asking. Is your mother ok?"

He took a deep breath then paused for a minute before he finally said, "Yea she' fine she's somewhere strung out god knows what. We usually see her once a month if that. We've been staying with my grandmother since she found out we were living on the streets," he confessed to me and it just broke my heart.

"If you would like, you're Hectors child therefore you're my child as well. You are more then welcome to stay with us while we either buy you a home or get one build that will be perfect for you and your sisters. As long as Hector and I are breathing you and your sisters will be fine. I just wish he would have told me about you earlier," I said finally pulling up to the house. The way he looked at the house tickled me but also made me feel bad because Hector had not been taking care of him. His mouth was in the O shape as he was surprised at how big it was.

"It's your home now so get use to it. Tomorrow when you drunken father wake up we can go look for you one ok," I told him.

His cheeks turned red and he said, "Yes ma'am."

"Jigsaw no need to be embarrassed. I'm mad at the fact your

father hasn't been taking care of you. You will get use to this life in no time. I will set up accounts for you and your sisters tonight so you all can go shopping tomorrow too," I told him.

When he reached up and hugged me I knew then just how much he was going to appreciate everything we were going to be doing for him. Brooklyn was so spoiled she would just spend whatever without asking but that was our fault. That girl could spend 10,000 a day and that was a slow day for her. The day her dad called me talking about her mini shopping sprees and he needed more work I dived back in the game head first and meet Lucas father and got them connected. Since then he's been doing great.

Once I showed Jigsaw where he and the girls would be sleeping we got Hector in the shower and when he woke up from the cold water we couldn't do anything but laugh. Even though today was a sad day it made me smile because he was still himself despite the pain he was in and I think having Jigsaw there was helping as well.

The next morning while everyone was still asleep I woke up and went to the store. I had to get some things to make breakfast because I knew the girls would be hungry. I fixed pancakes, sausage, eggs, grits, bacon, and hash browns. Once I finished I guess everyone smelled the food because they all came straight to the kitchen.

Hector was the last one to come in the kitchen and when he did you could feel his energy and also tell that he was hiding his hurt. With him being my husband I knew him like the back of my hand. "Good morning," I told everyone as I passed plates around the table. When everyone said good morning back we dived into the food. I told Hector about the information on Jigsaw mom and his situation and he became so mad at himself I had to pour all the liquor in the house down the sink.

Today we were going shopping and picking out furniture for the kids. I also had a plan on getting Jigsaw in school too since he had to drop out to take care of his sisters. As long as we were here their education was coming first. The girls were going to go to Franklin Road Academy and Jigsaw was going to go there too but they will have to test him first to see how far behind he is. Since it's the summer I was going to get them all set up with the best tutors ever.

We hit so many stores today I'm sure our bank account was like bitch stop spending money but oh well. When Brooklyn died yesterday I was feeling so lonely but now I wasn't. When I say we shopped till we dropped we did. I don't ever think I heard thank you so much in my life until today. Jigsaw and his sisters put life back into me and I was forever thankful for how happy they were making us and they didn't even know it.

• •

Hector

One the outside I looked fine, but on the inside I was slowly dying. I lost my only baby girl and granddaughter and didn't know what to do right now. Poppy was suppose to be hitting my house looking for my stash but when he found out Brooklyn died he had a change of heart. Now I'm far from stupid if he thought I was going to believe that shit. I was simply playing my part and also keeping my guard up. I lost one child but gained 3 more when Jigsaw and his sisters came into my life. When Bella told me how they were living and that Jigsaw dropped out of school to take care of them sent me over the edge.

Right now I was headed to find Tracey cracked out ass so she could sign her rights over. I don't even see how the school system even let him drop out when he was only 16 years old. The more Bella told me about his past the more it pissed me of cause I wasn't there for him. Now I was thankful Tracey never tried to sell the kids to get her fix.

When I put word out I was looking for her I got a phone call within 10 minutes saying she was over off Jefferson St. I pulled up in my all black Chevy Tahoe and blew my horn at her. "Can I help you?" she asked when she came to the window. I hit the door locks an she climbed right inside and I pulled of from the curb.

"Tracey why you never told me I had a son by you? You knew I would have taking care of him and your girls if you needed the help," I preached to her and shook my head.

"Well Hector you were married and I didn't want Bella beating my ass again," she said to me while holding her head down in shame.

"Well she knows and she's mad that you didn't come to us sooner. Did you know Jigsaw dropped out of school? That boy is smart as hell and he's picking up the slack I should be doing. The kids are staying with me so I would love it if you signed your right over," I said while passing her the paperwork and a pen. She looked at the paper then signed it.

Against my better judgment I tossed her some cash so she could eat because she looked like she hadn't eaten in days. When she exited my truck I pulled off an headed to make a few stops before I went home. I had to get Jigsaw a phone and pick up bikes for his baby sisters which were now my daughters as well. I thought she would fight me for the rights but she just gave them to me with no problem.

When I arrived back to the house the kids were in the pool and Bella was sun bathing, but I think she was crying because her eyes were puffy as far as I could see. "Are you okay?" I asked while sitting down right next to her. The moment she took off her oversized Dior sunglasses I knew the answer to my own question.

"Tracey gave us full rights of all the kids."

"Well that was easy, I thought she would have put up a fight."

"Me too Bella, but it's to the point that she's so far gone I think she knew what was best for them. She also said she didn't come to us sooner because she thought you would beat her ass again since I cheated with her," I truthfully told her.

The look that she gave me was funny because it was proof that she would have beat her ass too. "Have the kids talked about their mom since they've been here?"

"Hector you know damn well they haven't. Jigsaw said they haven't seen her in a month. I honestly don't think they care for her anymore." When Bella told me that it really made wonder on why she signed the papers so quick. Bella also found out Tracey only saw the kids like once every two to three months if that. These kids needed a family and that's what I was going to give them. I lost one daughter and now that I had gained two I was not going to let them make the same mistake that Brooklyn did and let a boy drag her to her death.

CHAPTER 12: THE DAY THE EARTH STOOD STILL

Jigsaw

    Growing up life was never easy for me. My mom was a crackhead and had always told me my father was dead when truth be told he was the biggest dope dealer in town. When Lucas found me and saw that I was looking for work to feed my baby sisters he gave me a job, but Brooklyn had that snatched away from me when she killed him. Luckily I found out she was my sister and who my real father was and now that's who we are living with.

    My mom only cared for herself and her fix. She never did try to sale us to get her fix but she did fuck anything to get it. One night she came home and told us to pack everything we had to go. I didn't know where we were going to go cause we had no family to depend on. We roamed the streets for weeks until Ms. Hattie the candy lady found us sleeping on the playground one night took us in. I had already dropped out of school so I always went looking for work during the day.

I had lucked up on finding Lucas a few months back when the niggas in the hood were clowning me about my shoes. Any money I made I always spent on my sisters so I never cared for how I looked. He saw the determination in my eyes and gave me a job the same day. All the money he gave me went on clothes, shoes, food, and any items my sisters needed. I also helped Ms. Hatti pay her bills even though she always refused the money.

The night Bella asked us to stay I was more then happy to help. Hector even liked having us around. I found out my mom signed her rights over to them so now they were our parents and I was glad we were in a loving home.

The first night in the home I told Bella everything that we had been through and she promised we never had to worrying about anything ever again. She even said they would build us our own home but I told her I was only 18 and that I was not ready for that. They got us enrolled into private school and also got me the best tutor so I could get caught up before the summer was over with.

Today was the day of Brooklyn, Lucas, and baby B's funeral. That morning seemed as if the Earth had stood still. My father had not said a single word to anyone that morning. Bella and I had to actually get him dressed because he wouldn't even move. My father and I were both dressed in our matching black Tom Ford suits, with our white button down shirt, and a black tie. Bella and the girl wore all black Dior dresses with gold Dior sandals. I never really got to know my sister and it actually makes me fell bad even though it wasn't my fault.

"Hey Bella the cars have arrived," I told her as I went to

make sure the girls were still dressed. One by one we all piled into the limo and headed to the church. When we arrived at the church you would have thought Michael Jackson was in town to do a concert it was so packed. I can say my family had plenty of support right now. For some odd reason I felt as if something was off.

When we walked inside everyone looked as if they had saw a ghost when they say me with Bella and Hector. "When this is over I will take you to the warehouse. We have some business to handle," Hector whispered into my ear. I already knew what that meant. We had Zack and Sade still tied up. Hell I don't even know if they were still alive or not. Nobody had went to check on them since they found Nessa and Brooklyn almost beat to death. When the funeral was over we headed to the cemetery for the burial.

I felt like someone was watching us and I had to bring it to Hector's attention without causing so much commotion. "Are you okay son?" Hector finally asked because my eyes had been glued to the window the entire ride.

"I feel like something ain't right," I finally told him as I scooted closer to him so the girls wouldn't hear.

"You know, you're sister you to say the same thing and was always right," he said while passing me his 9. I put it into my suit pocket and went back to watching our surroundings. By the time we reached the graveyard it was as if the security had tripled.

"I lost one child and I don't plan on losing another one," he told me as we got out of the car. We both helped Bella over to the grave because she could barely hold it together. You wouldn't know because of the shades and hat hiding her face. We let the girls sit as we stood looking around waiting for someone to jump stupid. "Hey pops you see that girl in the back. Her name is Raven, she approached me the other day asking about Lucas and Brooklyn the night we left Ms. Hatti house," I told him while keeping my eyes locked on her.

"That's Lucas ex. She had a baby by his homeboy and stated stalking him. I'm not sure what she wanted but trail her when we leave and see where she goes," then passed me the keys to the truck that one of the security guards were driving.

Throughout the entire service Raven was taking pictures and constantly answering her phone as if she was giving someone the location to where we were. Either way I was ready for whatever dumb shit she tried to play. Once it was over she made her way over to me while I was calling Hector. "Hey I'm not sure if you remember me but my name is Raven. I asked you about Lucas not to long ago. Are you holding up okay?"

"Nah, I don't remember you but I could get to know you if you're up for it," hoping she took my bait.
"I just wanted to make sure you were ok. I knew he was your friend and all so I was just checking on you. If you want you can come to my house afterwards and I can make you feel better," she said while licking my earlobe. I thought with my dick because I said,

"Sure I will stop by. Here let me see your phone so I can put my number in it and you can send me your address."

The entire time I was wondering how someone could be so dumb. I could have killed her right here but I didn't know who she had come with. What she didn't realize was that when I put my number in her phone I slide a tracker on it to see where she went. You see they didn't call me Jigsaw for no reason. I was the best hacker around. You could give me any puzzle and I would answer it in under 30 seconds flat.

I really didn't have to follow her home but I was going to do it anyway. I wrote down every address she went to and how long she was there too. This one address she kept going back to so I quickly sent it over to Hector to find out who lived here. When he told me it was Poppy address we knew then what she wanted. I was still going to play along to see what they were up to.

That night she sent me Poppy's address so of course I wasn't going alone. When I told my dad he had people sat up in every house surrounding that one. We even had a maid on the inside feeding us the information that we needed too. "You don't have to do this if you don't want to son."

"I have to dad. Did you ever think that Brooklyn probably killed her self for other reasons. I mean let's be real, she said Roxi's child was Lucas child but no one has found this child. What if she didn't even mean to pull trigger. What if the bullet came from inside the house, like did y'all ever test the bullet?"

From the stories I've heard about my sister I can't see her killing herself knowing she was pregnant and had everything she wanted at her finger tips. I mean everyone wanted her dead for a reason but what was the reason behind it. I needed answers and I wanted them now. When my father didn't answer I took that as my que to head out.

When I arrived I spotted someone in almost every window of the house. My father made sure I had a bullet proof vest on before I left so since I had a suit on you couldn't even tell. I had a 9 in each pocket of the inside of my jacket. I wasn't going into this house unprotected period. If I didn't trust you I never would. I knocked on the door waiting for someone to come to it. I started to walk off until Raven finally answered the door.

"I'm so sorry about that. My father was holding me hostage. He wanted to meet you but I told him no," she said as she pulled me into the house and up to her room.

"No offense I would like to meet him. I mean this is his house. You never step foot into another mans home without speaking to him," I preached to her then left out her room. I could tell she was use to dealing with fuck boys because she didn't have anything else to say.

She lead me to an office to finally meet her father. "It's nice to meet you sir. My name is Larry," I said while extending my hand.

"It's nice to meet you Larry. My name is Roman. I hear you're hear to take my daughter out. I asked that you have her back home before curfew and you will be just fine with me," he said while shaking my hand.

"Will do sir," I told him as she pulled me out the office towards the front door.

"Where's your restroom?"

"Two doors to the left. I will meet you on the front porch."

The moment I went to the restroom I went looking for a place to hide my jammer and the device I needed to hack every computer in here. I chose to hide it in the air vent because from the looks of it they don't clean it and would never think to look there. When I finished I headed to my truck to see where we were headed to. This chick was dumb if she thought I would believe that she lived with her father. She actually lived on the other side of town with her son so she was raising red flags to me already.

I sent a quick text to my father letting him know I was headed there to have everything ready. Brian had already jammed the signal to Roman's house and was getting all of the necessary information that we needed right now. I took the long way home even though she had never been to Hectors house. "You live here alone," she asked while staring at the home.

"No I live here with my father, step mother, and two baby sisters. Everyone is at a party right now so we have the place to ourselves right now."

Once inside we went upstairs to my room. She wanted a tour but I told her I would give her one before we left. Truth is, everyone is downstairs in the office going through and everything they could find on the devices at Roman's house.

"What does your father do for a living?"

"He does real-estate, and has a grass cutting service. My step mother is a lawyer, and also owns a few business," I lied straight through my teeth. Raven didn't know that I was Brooklyn sister because if she did she would have never came over. When I got the text from Brian said they had everything they needed I could kill her now.

I lead her to a room that was being redone but gave a view to the pool in the backyard. "Your fathers name is Roman huh?"

"Ye-yeah it is why you ask," she stuttered.

"No reason. He just looked like I had seen him somewhere before that's all."

"Oh I doubt you know my father he just moved back in town a few weeks ago when his brother died."

"You mean Javier."

When she tried to run I snatched her back by her ponytail. Her cries did nothing to me because all my life I was taught person whos cries is weak and has been caught lying.

"Please don't hurt me. I'm only doing what my father told me to do,"

"No you're doing what you want to do Raven. You see I know more about you then you think. I know you're Lucas ex. You have a son with a guy named Reggie. Roman's real name is Julio. Your father whos also my uncle, is trying to take down their brother Hector which is my father. You can put the phone away the signal is jammed," I said while watching her look for a way out.

"Look you got me. But see I also have a tracker they are headed here now. So if I don't text him in the next 30 minutes they will come looking for me here,"

"You mean the tracker I took off your phone the moment we got in the car and you were busy fixing your make up. It's sitting in the street in front of Kobe Steak House so good luck with that." *Spat!!!* Was the sound my gun made when I pulled the trigger.

I put her body into a suitcase and threw it in the back of my truck. "Have they secured her fathers home pops?"

"Yes they have. You sure you want to do this?"

"Dad I got this. The signal to their house is jammed so they can't call for help if they wanted to. If they did any call, text message, and email will be routed to a throw away phone. Dad I'm not a slouch I'm smarter then you think. Just because I dropped out of school doesn't mean anything. I do a lot of research in my spare time."

"You take the lead we are not that fair behind you ok."

"Alright pops."

Ten minutes later I was pulling out the drive way headed to Julio's house. This beef started all because their brother wouldn't hand the family business over to them and because they were all money hungry. If money makes you turn on blood then you have no ounce of loyalty in your body. When I arrived back to my uncles house I let myself in this time. I hacked his security footage so it was looping and he didn't see anything that was going on right now.

"I brought your daughter back home she's upstairs in her room," I lied to him.

"Alright son. You know I like you because you respect my rules."

"I was raised by a lady who always sad a man shows respect any woman and never put their hands on them," I told him.

"She was a smart woman. Too bad she didn't teach you to learn when you were in the presence of an enemy."

"You see Julio my father, your brother actually taught me that. To bad you didn't learn from him and to not use his son against him. Tell Javier I said hello," just as I popped him in both his knees so he couldn't run.

"Burn in hell bitch,"

When I walked out the house went up in flames. Their was a side of me that no one knew about. It was a side that was tired of everyone getting over on me. Lucas had put me up on so much game that I was teaching my father some new things. Finally ever enemy we had was now dead. Poppy thought he could hide out in his basement he was dead wrong. We leaked fumes in there so the poison killed him and if it didn't the fire would. The ride home was a quiet one because I had just caught my first few bodies for my father and I was sure these wouldn't be the last of them.

I went straight to the shower to get all the dirt that was on me off. I scrubbed my body and washed my hands in bleach to wash all of Ravens DNA off of me. The screams of my step mother interrupted my shower. I quickly grabbed my towel and raced downstairs.

"Bella are you okay?"

"Jigsaw do you believe in ghost?"

"No ma'am. Is there a reason why I should?"

"No it's okay it was just a bad dream I guess. You can go back to bed down."

That night I tossed and turned because I couldn't sleep. Who knew that catching your first few bodies would have your mind all over the place. Here it is going on 4am and I couldn't sleep for shit. I finally drifted to sleep and started to dream: *"It's alright that you can't sleep. I was the same way when I caught my first body. You have to put the feelings in the back of your head if not it will drive you crazy. My father taught me a lot of things growing up and so did your father. Make sure you give him a chance and don't go to hard on him. If he had known about you sooner you would've been there but I didn't. Tell your dad Brooklyn is doing just find and that he needs to let her go. We will always watch over y'all. If you ever want to talk you know were to find me.*

I woke up in a cold sweat because the dream felt so real. I noticed it was going on 10am and everyone was still asleep so I headed to the cemetery. I sat next to the dirt pile and just started talking. Lucas was the only person I had ever known that gave me a chance. He was like the big brother I never had and I wish I could still talk to him. For the first time I broke down. Did I think I was weak no, but growing up anyone who ever helped me died and I didn't want to lose my father or my new step mother.

"Real thugs don't cry man," I heard a voice behind me say but never got up to turn around to see who it was.

"I'm just tired of losing people man. Everyone that ever helps me dies. I lost my big brother I always wished I had and I cant bring him back," I said. When I turned around to see who the mystery man was I had blacked out because I couldn't believe my eyes.

CHAPTER 13: DREAMS DO COME TRUE

Bella

When I got a phone call that Jigsaw was found in the cemetery unresponsive me and his father rushed to be by his side. We didn't want to tell the girls what had happened just yet so we let them sit in the lobby with our body guards while we headed back to check on him. I was the first to reach the room and immediately broke down in tears at the sight in front of me. "Bella what's wrong?" The only thing I could do was point because my emotions were everywhere.

Once I finally got myself together I hauled off and beat Lucas in his chest. "So who's genius idea was it for you two to fake your death?" I was so angry Hector could barley get me off of him.

"The only way we would have come out on top and unharmed was this way. The day we found Brooklyn in that basement I couldn't dare lose her or my baby to this shit. We had to do it because Julio wasn't going to stop."

"Where's Brooklyn and why didn't you warn us?"

"Because Bella we had to make it look as real as possible and she's over there sleep. Don't wake her grumpy ass up either," he said while pointing to the couch in the corner.

I walked over to here and placed my hand on her stomach. My granddaughter must have known it was me because she was going crazy. The moment Brooklyn woke up I pulled her into my arms and let the tears fall. "Oh I missed you so much why didn't y'all tell me about this plan?" I asked her.

"Ma we had to make it look as real as possible and well you cant act for shit. Dad sure did do a good job. That night you thought he was drunk he wasn't. He poured liquor on his shirt he had only dunk water that night. We've been at his mom's house the entire time. The entire time you thought he was getting drunk we were plotting on Julio in Lucas old room ma," she told me.

"I should beat the fuck out of all of y'all." I was so mad I left the room. After I checked on the girls I checked on jigsaw when they confirmed he would be fine I took the girls to get some food before I had smacked everyone in that room. The games were on if they thought they could pull a fast one on me. I guess they forget the jokes I use to play on them back in the day. The house was about to set up like a home alone trap and it was game on.

"Ma are you coking tonight?' Brooklyn asked as soon as I stepped back into the room. The evil grin that was on my face was to hard to smile but I did.

"Of course I will cook your favorite meal. Bring Jigsaw with y'all. Oh and your father to he's not riding home with me," I told them then left the room.

Brooklyn

To say that my mom was not mad was an understatement. He checks were so red we couldn't do anything but laugh after when she left out the room. I felt bad that we had to do my baby brother like that but we couldn't risk anyone slipping up and telling someone that we faked our death. My mom could not act for shit or hold water sometimes so we did what was best. Hell my dad agreed to it so she should be mad at him not us.

"Dad if mom poisons the food I will haunt you for the rest of my life," I said. He thought it was the funniest shit ever how she showed that evil grin but I didn't.

"Girl she isn't going to poison that food but that house about to be a death rap when we get there," he told me.

"The hell you mean a death trap?"

"Well let's just say when you play pranks or jokes on her she likes to play back," he said and I knew then we were fucked.

"So I guess I wasn't seeing ghost huh?" Jigsaw asked the second he woke up.

"Nope little brother. I'm sorry we had to do you like that but that was the only way we could get Poppy guard down and put him into hiding to get the real person behind this shit to come out. Lucas didn't want anything to happen to you the baby or me so he felt it was best but. We heard you was laying niggas out so how was it?" The look on his face told it all and I had to laugh.

"It was ok. I couldn't sleep last night truth be told."

"Yea the first time is always like that you will get over it, want he pops?" When our dad nodded his head yes Jigsaw just laughed.

When they checked his vitals we were clear to finally go home and be enemy free for the first time in years and it felt so damn good. In three weeks I would be having my daughter and me and Lucas had yet to come up with a name. I was glad we could come out the house because being coped up in the house with him for a week was starting to kill me. I loved my husband but that nigga had been in my face so much I couldn't even shit in peace.

"Dad did you tell Jig the good news yet?" I asked while smiling so hard.

"No he didn't what's the good news pops?" Jig asked while sitting up in the seat to hear us clearly.

"We have a trip with the connect in a few months and you're going with us because Brooklyn won't be able to fly out then. So the next few months before you start school you will have a lot to catch up on." I could tell Jig was excited and couldn't wait.

"That's what's up pops I'm ready."

"Here's the kicker part little bro. Y'all going to Costa Rica."

The smile he showed on his face could be seen for miles. I hated he had to grow up rough before our dad found out about him but now he was about to be exposed to a life of luxury. He could have anything he want with the snap of a finger and didn't even know it. When I finished showing Jig the ropes our dad was just going to have another spoiled kid on his hands. First I had to break my brother from his shyness when he was around the family.

When we got home we all had to creep through the house and walk on eggshells because mom was still mad. To be honest I didn't give a shit about her being mad, I mean it isn't my fault her ass can't act to save her fucking life. You could tell her to play dumb and she would do the complete opposite. Like you can play a fucking ghost just fine all my life but you get mad when we fake our death who does that.
"So are y'all doing playing dead?" Bella asked as soon as we walked into the kitchen. Without thinking twice I snapped.

"REALLY BELLA? REALLY? BECAUSE THE LAST TIME I CHECKED YOU'VE BEEN PLAYING A GHOST IN MY LIFE SINCE I WAS 8 FUCKING YEARS OLD. YOU WANT TO GET MAD AT ME BECAUSE WE DID WHAT WAS BEST SO ME AND THE BABY WOULD NOT BE HARMED AND THIS HOW YOU WANT TO ACT YOU CAN KISS MY ASS AND GO BACK TO BEING THE GHOST THAT YOU WERE. I NEVER ASKED FOR THIS FUCKING LIFE, THE FUCKING LIFE CHOSE ME. NOW GET THIS THROUGH YOUR HEAD I'M GROWN AS FUCK AND CAN DO AS I PLEASE. IF YOU WANTED TO CONTROL MY LIFE YOU SHOULDVE BEEN HERE WHEN I WAS YOUNGER!" I yelled at her.

I was so pissed I didn't even give her a chance to respond before I left the house. "I see we have a lot more in common then I thought," Jig said while walking up on me sitting on the balcony.

"Yea she use to be a shitty mom. She's trying to be one now but what she fails to realize is that I'm grown. She walked out on me and I guess she still thinks I'm 8 and I'm not."

"I know how you feel. My mom chose the rock over me and my sisters. It was hard until I finally found out who my father was.

All my life she told me he was dead when he really wasn't. I could hate her but I'm not because she thought me how to work for everything that I need and not take a single handle out."

"Yea you're right. I'm so spoiled I cry when I can't get my way. I wish I knew about you sooner because being the only child in the house growing up sucked."

I sat an talked to Jig for at least an hour before Lucas finally came out. "Brooklyn have you finally calmed down yet baby?" I rolled my eyes at him and turned my head. I liked when he use to chase me and now he doesn't do it anymore. I'm sure my dad has something to do with that.

"It took you long enough to come find me," I said smartly. At times I picked arguments with him just to fake cry so he could fuck my brains out and put me to sleep.

He took me by my hand and pulled me into the house into my old room and locked the door behind us. I could tell he was made but I didn't care. "Brooklyn I'm going to tell you this one time and one time only. Don't ever talk to your mom like that ever again in front of everyone you hear me." He said it so calmly I thought I was being punked for a minute.

"Yea I understand," I dryly said cause I really didn't care.

When he got it my face I almost smacked him until he grabbed my waist. "Don't get fucked up," he said and all I smelt was the peppermint on his breath. My mind quickly went into the gutter because the next thing I knew his tongue was in my mouth and we were undressing each other. His moms house was to quiet to have sex in but my dads wasn't it. You would just think the TV was up loud or the kids were playing and ignore the sounds.

"What if I want you to fuck me up," I said seductively. After he got my clothes off he laid me down on the bed and climbed on top of me.

"As you wish," he said then traced my body with his tongue until he reached my pearl. The tapping he was doing with his tongue was sending my body into overdrive and I was loving it. Since I've gotten further along it doesn't take me much to climax because my body was so ender right now.

"FFFFUCK!!!" I moaned as I climaxed in his mouth and he licked all my juices away.

He was scared that he would smash the baby so I got on my knees so I could get the best back shots in the world. He entered me slowly from behind and my knees started to buckle. "Naw what you doing? You clearly wanted this dick and now you're going to get it," he said in my ear while helping me back onto my knees. When he got back inside of me he used his right hand to massage my pussy and his left hand to hold my waist. The only sounds that could be herd in the room is our skin smacking up against each other. He was driving into me so fast he had to stop because he didn't want to nut yet.

"Somebody can't handle the pussy," I teased him. He laughed at me then gave me some shots so deadly I squirted all over he place. When he finally came he clasped right next to me on the bed breathing heavily.

"Brooklyn you know I love you but you need to cut your mom some slack. She did what she thought was best for your safety back then so take it easy on her. I'm sure she hates that she did that but she doesn't need you rubbing it in her face." When I thought about it he was actually telling the truth.

"I will go apologize, but first I need to shower." He went to turn it on then came and helped me out the bed. I felt like I was getting bigger over night because it was hard for me to move sometimes. Finally, an hour later we were out the shower and putting our pajamas on. Lucas stayed in the room while I went to go find my mom. When I went into her room she was already asleep so I went back into my old room and shut the door. "She's asleep." I told Lucas as I laid down next to him and put my head on his chest.

"Ok baby but make sure you tell her tomorrow ok."

"I will baby good night." When he kissed my head I jerked it back and kissed his lips. He couldn't do anything but laugh.

CHAPTER 14: A TRUE DIVA

Lucas (Two weeks Later)

The summer was finally over and we were about to take Jigsaw with us for the meeting so he could know how to handle things when we passed it all down to him. Brooklyn was upset that she couldn't come because she could have the baby at any moment and we still had not thought of a name. Plus the doctor said it was not safe for her to fly right now either. That morning she tried to suck the skin off my dick since we weren't having sex because she was so big now. I mean she did it so good she had put me back to sleep.

When I woke up she had everything packed and food cooked for me so that I could catch my flight in a few. She walking around the condo in nothing but her panties and her silk and she looked damn good. As she passed me I pulled her into my lap because I was going to miss her until I got back. "Is my baby going to be good while daddy is gone?" I said to her stomach but Brooklyn thought I was talking to her.

"Yes baby."

"Girl I'm talking to my princess not you. Yo ass ain't got a choice but to be good anyway." She hit me playfully and got up from my lap to finish cleaning the kitchen.

The moment I saw her slouch over in pain I started to cancel the meeting. "Baby are you ok?" I asked while running over to her side and helping her to the couch to have a seat.

"Yes I'm fine. She was probably sitting wrong like always." I had a feeling she was lying but I didn't want to start an argument with her.

"Are you sure. I can tell Hector I will sit this one out and stay home with you."

"No baby I will be fine. If you want tell mama to come sit over here with me." I looked her in the eyes and she was dead serious. This was going to be our biggest reup ever and that's probably why she didn't want me to miss it. I felt like as long as Hector and Jig went everything would be ok.

I quickly called my mom and she came right over so that I could meet them at the airport and head out. "Ma don't let her do anything ok. I been telling her all morning to sit down and she wont maybe she will listen to you." I told her as I kissed Brooklyn belly then her lips so I could go.

"Ma don't listen to him I'm fine I promise, but I do want you to stay cause she can come any day now and I don't want to be alone." When she told my mom that I almost dropped my bags until she told me to take my ass on.

"I love you baby. Call me if you need anything or if anything goes wrong and I mean anything." I demanded her.

"Ok daddy. We love you too." She said while rubbing her belly then sitting back down on the couch.

Soon as I hit the door I heard them start talking about baby names and I prayed the didn't come up with something ratchet or stupid. I caught a cab to the airport because I wasn't trying to find somewhere to park when I got there. It took the cabbie 30 minutes to reach the airport and when I did I paid the man and headed to check in. The lady who checked my bag on was trying to flirt with me until I showed her my wedding ring. What made is worse she kept trying it. I wish Brooklyn had dropped me of because she would have beat this girl ass pregnant and all.

I meet Hector and Jigsaw at the gate and he was looking more and more like his father everyday. He even acted like him. He was the quiet one out of the family and that was a good thing because you would think he was deaf until he read your body language and told you more about your self then you would even know. "You ready for your first trip?" I asked as I approached him and Hector.

"Ready as I will ever be big bro." He was the little brother I wished I had. Yeah Ricky was my brother but Jigsaw was my baby brother hell I'm married to his sister.

When we headed to the plane we greeted the piolet then took our seats on the jet. I texted Brooklyn to let her know we were getting on the plane that I would text her when we touched down and powered my phone off. "This is a 6 hour flight you might as well catch some sleep while you can." I told Jig as I grabbed a blanket and pillow out the closet. From the look on his face he was to excited to sleep so I let him be as he watched the plan take off I let the sleep take over my body.

Once we touched down I powered my phone back on and sent my wife a quick text.

Me: Just touched down. I love you!!!

Wifey: Ok baby. Be safe I love you too!!!

Me: How are you feeling?

Wifey: I'm ok. Ma sleeping so I'm about to take a nap.

Me: Ok love. Don't forget to call me if you need anything.

Wifey: I won't baby. Enjoy the trip.

    The last text she sent me I wanted to say I wanted to enjoy her but I was going to let her get all the sleep she needed. My mother was there with her and Nessa was going to go over there in the morning because that's when Marcus was due to be here with us. We headed straight to the hotel I went straight to sleep. These days I slept more than I was awake and everyone said I was nesting, whatever the hell that shit meant.

    When I woke up the next morning I realized I was almost late for the meeting. I jetted to the shower to get ready because I hated to be late. Hector and Jigsaw were already gone and told a car would be there for me in 15 minutes. I pulled my fitted Tom Ford suit out the closet and processed to get dressed. I finished getting dressed just as the driver pulled up.

Me: Good morning. How are my two favorite ladies?

Wifey: Good morning baby. We're doing fine just finished eating breakfast about to take a nap. How's our favorite man?

Me: Miserable because I'm not around you two. Text me when you wake up heading out now. I love y'all. Don't be afraid to call if you need to.

Wifey: We love you too baby. I won't.

I put my phone on vibrate just as we pulled up to the spot. We were on the rooftop of a restaurant waiting for Hendrix to meet us. Jig seemed to be enjoying Jamaica but I think he was enjoying the ladies instead. When Hendrix pulled up we stood to meet him then took our seats.

"How's the family?" he asked as soon as we sat down.

"Doing good and your?"

"Bring a pain in the ass," "I feel you on that, let's get started shall we."

• •
Brooklyn

After I texted Lucas I laid back down just as Nessa arrived. "Big mama. How's my god baby in there?"

"Girl she need to bring her ass on my back huts and all I do is sleep all day."

"Hell you did that before her." Nessa teased me but she was telling the truth. She grabbed her a plate as I went to sit on the couch and take a nap. It took me a minute to fall asleep but when I did I was out like a dead person.

"MA!!!" I yelled as a sharp pain woke me up out of my sleep.

"What's wrong baby?"

"My stomach hurts. This time the pain is much worse," I cried to her as the pain came again Just as I tried to move my water broke.

"Ok let's get you to the hospital she's trying to come now," she told me as Nessa ran to the room to grab our bags and my phone. We made it to the car then another sharp pain hit me again. "AGH," I screamed.

"Yea she's coming call Lucas Nessa cause she's not going to be able to talk right now," Ma told her.

I handed her my phone as she dialed his number. "AGH MA HURRY UP IT HURTS SO BAD," I yelled just as Lucas answered the phone.

"Lucas it's time. She's in labor," Nessa told him. She handed me the phone and I just knew his ass was going to want to talk to me while I was in pain.

"Baby I'm on my way. Don't push her out until I get there ok."

"LUCAS LEE JENKIS IF YOUR ASS AINT HERE BY THE TIME I PUSH THAT'S YOUR FAULT. THIS SHIT HURTS BAD PLEASE GET HERE NOW. I SHOULD HAVE LET YOU STAY HOME," I cried into the phone.

I could hear that he was scared as he told my father and Hendrix that I was in labor. They both congratulated him and told him to go so get could get to me. Another contraction was coming as I was screaming into the phone at Lucas that it was his fault. He was getting on the jet the second we arrived to the hospital.

"Baby I'm on my way. The plane is about to take off. I have to hang up. I love you. Don't push my daughter out until I get there either," he demanded me then hung up the phone not giving me a chance to say anything back.

We headed to labor and delivery floor at Centennial Women's Hospital and they quickly put me in a room. They hooked me up to everything and check me. The nurse told me I had only dilated to 4 and had to go to 10 before I could push.

"How long will that take?" I asked.

"It could take you anywhere from 2-17 hours," she told me and I wanted to cry.

"Can I take something for the pain?"

"Yes ma'am. We will get the epidural started.

Once that was in me I felt like I was on a cloud. Since Lucas has a 6 hour flight to get to me I opted to sleep it away. I went from being in pain to not feeling anything all within an hour and I was loving that. When I found out I couldn't eat I almost lost it. I quickly went to sleep to not think about food because this was going to suck.

The doctors walking in and out of the room woke me up and I was so irritated and ready to snap but they were just doing their job. I pulled the cover over my head just as my room door opened again for what seemed like the 400th time.

"I know damn well you haven't push my daughter out yet." Lucas said as soon as he walked in. I rolled my eyes and pulled the cover off my face until I was hit with balloons, some pink roses, a big as teddy bear, and my man in the suit I loved on him the most.

"No. I think she was waiting for you to get here." I told him as he came and gave me a kiss.

I was staring at him like he was a piece of meat and he knew it. "Woman stop looking at me like that."

"You lucky I'm pregnant cause if I weren't I damn sholl would have been just now," I said and everyone started laughing.

"Girl stop. Where your moms?"

"She's in the food court. The girls got hungry so she had to go feed them."

"How much longer do you have before you can push my baby out?"

"I don't know go find the nurse and asked her."

I guess he thought I was being smart and I wasn't so I had to laugh at him for that attitude he had just caught. "What's so funny?"

"You and that attitude you have baby. But honestly I don't know the nurse said it could take anywhere from 2-17 hours." I finally told him.

"Oh okay. What's that number?" "

Which one baby?" I asked because it was so many on the screen popping up.

"Oh that's the baby heart beat why?"

"Is it suppose to go up and down like that?"

"I don't think so. Somebody go get the nurse,"

Just as I said the nurse came rushing into the room with the doctors on her heals. "Ok Brooklyn, we are going to have to do an emergency C-section because the baby's heart is dropping. Only one person can come back so whos going with you?"

"I will. I'm her husband," Lucas said before I even had the chance to answer it myself.

"Okay go with her so she can get you in the right clothing to go into the operating room with." The nurse begin unplugging me from all the machines then rolled me out of the room in the bed.

When I got to the OR room I was a nervous wreck. The room was cold and I was all alone while the nurses moved around the room setting everything up. After everything was ready they finally brought Lucas into the room and I was no longer scared anymore. "Are you ready?" the doctor asked me as they put a blue sheet up over my face.

"Yes. I'm ready." When they were sure I couldn't feel anything they cut me open and went to work.

Lucas held onto my hand for dear life. "Are you okay baby?"

"Yea I'm ok. I missed you. I think you were right about staying home too."

"True but I think she wanted to wait till her father got here anyway," he teased me. We both knew she was going to be a daddies girl because of how wild she went whenever he touched me belly.

"Alright dad. If you want you can stand up and watch. We are about to pull her out," the doctor told him.

Just as he stood up his face expression caused me to laugh. I don't think he like what he saw not one bit. When they finally pulled her out of me Lucas passed out. I rolled my eyes at how dramatic he was until the nurses had to help him out the room. "Is my baby ok?" I asked because I didn't hear her crying. When I caught a glimpse of her she was blue. I started crying because I feared the worst. They took her out the room while doing cpr on her. I felt like my life was being tuned upside down.

Once I was stitched up they tried to calm me down but nothing was helping. When Lucas got back in the room I couldn't even tell him what was wrong. When he finally got me calmed down they explained everything that was going on. "When we pulled her out her umbilical cord was wrapped around her neck and she wasn't breathing. We have her stable and she is find and is breathing on her own now," the doctor finally told us.

"Can I see her?" I asked.

"Yes as soon as we get you back to your room we will bring her in there to you."

The second they put me in the room they brought us our baby girl and I couldn't help the emotions that came over me. "Girl if yo crybaby ass don't stop all of that crying," Lucas teased me.

"Baby shut up. I'm just happy," I told him but I'm sure he already knew that. When he placed her in my arms I fell in love at the first sight. My family was finally complete and we were living enemy free. Lucas went and got everyone and brought them into the room to finally meet baby Brooke Jenkins.

Finally a week later we were heading home to start on this new path called parenting. Since I had her Lucas had been such a big help. He handled his business from home since I was still in a lot of pain from the C-section that I had. We took shifts on who would wake up to feed her at night and it was usually him since he was always awake at crazy ass hours.

"Baby where are you going?" I asked him when he got out the shower.

"To the store. Do you need me to get you anything?"

"No I'm fine. Just bring me a few bottles and set them on the night stand so I wont have to move that far to get them." He quickly got some stuff for the baby and sat it all on the night stand and kissed me on my forehead.

"I love you baby I will be right back," he said as he kissed my forehead then left. I put some pillows on the other side of the baby then went back to the sleep because I was still tired.

CHAPTER 15: THIS IS IT
Lucas

It had been six months since we had baby Brooke and today was the day Brooklyn was getting her actual wedding. I had been up all night making sure everything was ready and perfect for her. This morning I sent her off to get her hair and nails done. My mom had the baby and Jigsaw was with me headed to the church.

Once inside and we saw that everything was ready we headed to the back room to get changed. "I know y'all are already married but are you nervous?" Jigsaw asked me.

"Hell yea. Nervous is an understatement right now. Me and you sister have our days to were I want to strangle her but I can't live without her. We could get married every year and I will always be nervous until I lay my eyes on her." I told him.

He knew I loved his sister and would do anything to protect her and baby Brooke. I noticed she looked like the perfect combo of me and Brooklyn everyday. I took her birth control pills and swapped them out for tic tac because I wanted a son bad. She kept saying she wanted to wait but I wasn't having that. We I looked at my watch I noticed it was almost time to start so I headed with to take my spot at the top of the church with my best man Zack. Yea we sat down and talked and he told me everything not leaving anything out. He even told me where Javier, Julio and Poppy had their stashes at so we got it all and split it down the middle.

We were flowing in so much dough we didn't even know what the hell to do with the shit now. After the wedding we were moving to Italy for the summer. When Brooklyn came into my view and started walking down the aisle I couldn't help but to shed a few tears. My baby was the most beautiful woman I had ever meet. I felt like I won the lottery when I was with her and I never wanted that feeling to fade.

Once the ceremony was over we headed straight to the airport. The after party was taking place in Italy and we paid for everyone to travel with us. When we arrived to the airport we got some many congratulations I got tired of saying thank you. Brooklyn and I took my private jet while everyone else took the other jet. When we lifted off we went into the room in the back and made the love the entire way to Italy.

If she wasn't pregnant by the time we got off this plane she was going to be when we got to Italy. I wanted so many kids with her but she swore Brooke was enough by her self when she really wasn't. "You ready?" I asked her as she was waking up out of her sleep.

"You know I'm always ready when it comes to you daddy," she said while kissing me and mounting my dick one last time before we landed.

• •

Brooklyn

Today had be the best day of my life. I got the wedding of my dreams and now I was headed to Italy for my reception with my entire family. The entire flight we made love. For some reason I just could not get enough of him. When we landed we headed straight to the hotel where our reception was being held.

Once we walked in the crowd erupted with cheers. As I looked around the room I was happy to see my friends. Lucas even made sure Carter, Elijah, and Egypt were there. When the blood test came back that they didn't belong to my father the state took them away and I had been sick behind that. Some how Lucas pulled some strings and here they were and boy did I miss them. Egypt was in love with Brooke, while carter and Elijah were to busy eating.

"Well baby girl I finally have to cut you off now," my dad told me while walking up beside me.

"Why," I asked with my puppy dog face hoping he would change his mind.

"I got custody of Carter, Elijah, and Egypt. I have a house full of girls and a spoiled granddaughter to take care of now," when he told me that I started crying teats of joy. Wow my family was really complete.

After we had our first dance it was time for the toast. Once everyone else had said their speeches it was time for me and Lucas to do ours and Lucas went first.

"To my wonderful beautiful wife. Mrs. Jenkins bring yo fine ass here girl. Since the day I first meet you I always knew that I would marry you. From our first fight to our first argument to our first kiss if I could it all over again I would always chose you. You're the one I run to when I'm having a bad day because you always know how to make it better. You saw the best in me when everyone else only saw the worst in me. You motivate me in more ways then you would ever know. Every morning when I wake up I always wonder how I can make your day better and you always say it's better because you're here. Whenever I'm sick you're always the best doctor in town for me when I went broke you never switched up on me and that's as real as it get. Baby you're the realist one on my team and until I leave this Earth you don't have to worry about a damn thing other then having more of my kids. I'm saying all of this to say Brooklyn Taylor Jenkins I love you girl and I ain't never gone stop loving you." When he did his speech is was not a single dry face in the crowd. That man sure knew how to put his words together. To know I was finally spending the rest of my life with him made me the happiest woman alive.

"Alright I want to thank you all for your support for my family and myself. The first time I laid eyes on Lucas I always said one day he would be mine now look at us. He's stuck with me for life now. Our road here wasn't easy but we made it. If I could go back in time to change anything I wouldn't because everything we went through only made us stronger. Lucas you are my homie, my lover, my bestfriend you name it it's you. You're patient with me when I have the worst attitudes on Earth. You know you're my number 1 and I'm you're number 1. We're stuck for life baby. I said I want this for life and I do. You make me feel complete in so many ways I couldn't thank you enough. I will never give you up and I really don't know how I could ever thank you enough. I want to show you how much I appreciate you. I want to think you for my gifts but it seems like you forgot one. I grabbed it out the car when we got here," I said as he walked over to me looking confused as ever.

He looked from me to the bag then asked, "What is it?"

"Boy if you don't open it and stop asking." He pulled a silver box out of the bag while everybody waited for him to open it.

"Boy you better hurry up before I snatch it and open it," yelled Zack and everyone started laughing. When he opened the box he immediately closed it and started crying. He picked me up spinning me around in circles kissing me all over my face. "Nigga what she get you." said his brother Ricky.

He took the mic out my hand and yelled, "SHE'S HAVING MY SON."

The end.

EPILOGUE

5 years later

Zack

The past 5 years of my life have been crazy. Me and Lucas were able to get past everything once I told him what happend. I was never a snake and it took him sitting down with me to find everything out. Once we got that all out the way it was as if nothing ever happend.

"Daddy I'm hungry!"

"Let's go get something to eat baby girl." I expressed to my daughter Miracle. and before you ask yes she belongs to Sade. After everything went done Sade couldn't cope. She ended up killing herself 2 months after we had Miracle. She isn't pose to even be here because she was born 3 months early but here she is still alive and looking just like her mother.

Everyday I kick my ass for not getting her the help I knew she needed. It was almost close to her death date and I hate this time of the year.

"Zake!" I heard my sister yell as I walked through her front door.

"What up sis?" I spoke to Brooke when she finally came into my view pregnant as ever. Yes Lucas knocked her up again. This was baby number 3 for them.

"How you holding up?"

"I'm good! How about you?"

"I'm perfect. My cousin Kahalid from Atl is on his way over with his wife and kids. Put Mirical down and let her play with the kids. The men are in the basement!"

As I headed to the basement I realized that even though I no longer has Sade I still had a family here to support us. I'll explain my story one day but for now it's about my sis and bro so I'm out.

Lucas

I was chilling in my man cave just as my brother Zake came in. Ever since Sade killed herself he's been going through it so I'm making his ass start therapy soon because my goddaughter didn't need to grow up with no parents at all.

Walking into my office in the basement, I looked over the security cameras and watched my wife walk around and stopping every few minuts. "I think Brooke's ass is in labor. Y'all look at this shit," I laughed while showing them the camera.

"Here ass trying to go natural again?"

"As always Ricky! She better not start that crying shit when it's too late to go to the hospital," I spat while lighting my blunt. We hit our 5 year mark in our marriage and I was still loving being married to Brooklyn. No matter how many fights we had I'm glad to say she's never went to bed mad.

"I got 10 bands that she fina call and tell you to take her to the hospital!" Ricky yelled as we watched her pick up her phone.

"I got 20 she fina call mama and lie first!" I cracked back.

When my phone didn't ring we kept watching. The second she hung up my mom was calling me. "LUCAS LEE JENKINS IF YOU DON'T GET YOUR WIFE TO THE HOSPITAL NOW AND STOP WATCHING HER ON CAMERA IN PAIN IMA BEAT THE BLACK OFF YO UGLY ASS. RICKY PAY UP MUTHAFUCKA YOU LOST!" my mom yelled then hung up

"What the fuck?" Ricky barked while handing me my money.

"I told you so!"

"How did you know she was gonna do that?"

"She been doing that shit since we got married! Let me get her to the hosptail," I told Ricky then walked off.

When I got upstairs she aleady had her bags by the door. "You ready?" I asked as I helped her to the truck.

"Ready as I'll ever be!" Let's go have your last kid ever!"

"Yeah whatever!" I huffed because she had me fucked up. I wanted a house full of kids and she thought she was about to stop now. She got me fucked up y'all.

"I love you LUCAS LEE JENKINS!"

"I love you too BROOKLYN TAYLOR JENKINS!"

When we got to the hospital it was like everyhting happend so fast and my second princess was born.

Brooklyn

Here we are 5 years later and I just gave birth to our final child. Lucas had me bent if he thought I was going to keep having kids. What he didn't know was that I got fixed because for now my three were enough. Plus i always had Jig twin sisters since he was running everything now.

I loved my new found sisters as if we had the same parents.

My life was finally complete after all these years. I lost my best freind Sade due to depression which caused me to have a miscarriage before I had this beautiful bundle of joy.

"How's Sade Marie?" Lucas asked as he walked back into the room while I was brestfeeding her.

"She's hungry as hell!" I informed him as he gave me my drink so I could have a sip.

"Brooklyn? Are you happy?" Lucas asked me out of the blue.

"Now you know I am! We might have our days but I can honeslty say our love never fades. We made it 5 years in marriage and you know what they say?"

"Naw what they say?" he asked while kicking off his shoes and climbing in bed with me.

"Once you make it to year 5 you gotta buy me whatever I want!"

"Oh really! Well what does my Queen want?"

"Nobody but you kissing on my tattoes," I cooed in his year as he kissed me and grabbed Sade from me. My life was offically perfect as I watched Lucas burp Sade. I had to snap a picture and post it on facebook with the caption "Even in my darkest days Sade Marie makes it all better! R.I.P. besite! #LongLiveSade" and my comments and likes went wild. I hide this pregnancy because of health issues but now I was ready to share the world with her.

"Mrs. Jenkins will you marry me again?"

"You know I will Mr. Jenkins!"

The end............. but we will be back soon.